About the Author

HASSAN BLASIM is a poet, filmmaker and short story writer. Born in Baghdad in 1973, he studied at the city's Academy of Cinematic Arts, where two of his films 'Gardenia' (screenplay and director) and 'White Clay' (screenplay) won the Academy's Festival Award for Best Work in their respective years. In 1998 he left Baghdad for Sulaymaniya (Iraqi Kurdistan), where he continued to make films, including the feature-length drama *Wounded Camera*, under the pseudonym Ouazad Osman, fearing for his family back in Baghdad under the Hussein dictatorship. In 2004, he moved to Finland, where he continues to make films. Hassan's stories first appeared in Arabic on www.iraqstory.com and his essays on cinema have featured in *Cinema Booklets* (Emirates Cultural Foundation). His first short story to be published in English was commissioned for *Madinah: City Stories from the Middle East* (Comma 2008). This, his first book, has been translated into five languages. His second, *The Iraqi Christ* (also translated by Jonathan Wright) was published by Comma in 2013. A selection of stories from both collections, titled *The Corpse Exhibition*, was published in the US, by Penguin in 2014.

Praise for Hassan Blasim's work:

'Dark, bitterly funny Borgesian tales...'
– The Chicago Tribune

'The existence of this book is reason for hope, proof of the power of storytelling.' – The Boston Globe

'Brutal, vulgar, imaginative, and unerringly captivating... A searing, original portrait of Iraq.' – Publishers Weekly

'Powerful, moving and deeply descriptive.' – Kirkus Reviews

'Blunt and gruesome.' – The Huffington Post

'Bolaño-esque in its visceral exuberance, and also Borgesian in its gnomic complexity... a master of metaphor.'
– The Guardian

'Blasim's vivid prose reflects the way the fantastic and the ordinary collapse into a Kafkaesque jumble during urban conflict.'
– The Financial Times

'Blasim's tone is a resilient blend of mordancy and broken lyricism.'
– Intelligent Life

'Blasim has been called, "the best writer of Arabic fiction alive". It is not his identity, however, but the quality of his writing that makes his voice striking. It is deeply troubling and complex, the metaphors arresting and violent.' – The Spectator

'An arrestingly vivid picture of the privation and the terrors of life in Iraq.' – Herald Scotland

THE MADMAN OF FREEDOM SQUARE

by
Hassan Blasim

Translated by Jonathan Wright

To my son, Ankido.

First published in Great Britain in 2009 by Comma Press
Second edition, 2014.
www.commapress.co.uk

'The Reality and the Record' was first published in *Madinah: City Stories from the Middle East* edited by Joumana Haddad (Comma, 2008).

Lines taken from *The Forgotten Language: An Introduction to the Understanding of Dreams, Fairy Tales and Myths* (New York: Rinehart & Co., Inc., 1951) by Erich Fromm are reprinted by permission. Lines taken from *Kierkegaard in Sicily* (Berlin: Matthes & Seitz, 2006) by Béla Hamvas are reprinted by permission.

A CIP catalogue record of this book is available from the British Library.

ISBN 1905583257
ISBN-13 978 1905583256

The publisher gratefully acknowledges assistance from the Arts Council England.
This book was a winner of an English Pen 'Writers in Translation' Prize 2009.
Comma gratefully acknowledges the support English Pen has given throughout.

FREEDOM
TO **WRITE**
FREEDOM
TO **READ**

Set in Bembo 11/13 by David Eckersall
Printed and bound in England by Berforts Information Press, Stevenage.

Contents

The Reality and the Record

EVERYONE STAYING AT the refugee reception centre has two stories – the real one and the one for the record. The stories for the record are the ones the new refugees tell to obtain the right to humanitarian asylum, written down in the immigration department and preserved in their private files. The real stories remain locked in the hearts of the refugees, for them to mull over in complete secrecy. That's not to say it's easy to tell the two stories apart. They merge and it becomes impossible to distinguish them. Two days ago a new Iraqi refugee arrived in Malmö in southern Sweden. He was in his late thirties. They took him to the reception centre and did some medical tests on him. Then they gave him a room, a bed, a towel, a bedsheet, a bar of soap, a knife, fork and spoon, and a cooking pot. Today the man is sitting in front of the immigration officer telling his story at amazing speed, while the immigration officer asks him to slow down as much as possible.

They told me they had sold me to another group and they were very cheerful. They stayed up all night drinking whiskey and laughing. They even invited me to join them in a drink but I declined and told them I was a religious man. They bought me new clothes, and that night they cooked me a chicken and served me fruit and sweets. It seems I fetched a good price. The leader of the group even shed real tears when he said goodbye. He embraced me like a brother.

'You're a very good man. I wish you all the best, and good luck in your life,' said the man with one eye.

I think I stayed with the first group just three months. They had kidnapped me on that cold accursed night. That was in the early winter of 2006. We had orders to go to the Tigris and it was the first time we had received instructions directly from the head of the Emergency Department in the hospital. At the bank of the river the policemen were standing around six headless bodies. The heads had been put in an empty flour sack in front of the bodies. The police guessed they were the bodies of some clerics. We had arrived late because of the heavy rain. The police piled the bodies onto the ambulance driven by my colleague Abu Salim and I carried the sack of heads to my ambulance. The streets were empty and the only sounds to break the forlorn silence of the Baghdad night were some gunshots in the distance and the noise of an American helicopter patrolling over the Green Zone. We set off along Abu Nawas Street towards Rashid Street, driving at medium speed because of the rain. I remembered the words the director of the Emergency Department in the hospital often used to say: 'When you're carrying an injured person or a patient close to death, the speed of the ambulance shows how humane and responsible you are. But when you are carrying severed heads in an ambulance, you needn't go faster than a hearse drawn by mules in a dark mediaeval forest.' The director saw himself as a philosopher and an artist, but 'born in the wrong country,' as he would say. He took his work seriously nonetheless and considered it a sacred duty, because to him running the ambulance section of the Emergency Department meant managing the dividing line between life and death. We called him the Professor and my other colleagues hated him and called him mad. I know why they hated him, because the enigmatic and aggressive way he spoke made him seem screwed up in the eyes of others. But I retained much respect and affection for him because of the beautiful and fascinating things he said. Once he said to me: 'Spilt blood and superstition are the basis of the world. Man is not the only

2

creature who kills for bread, or love, or power, because animals in the jungle do that in various ways, but he is the only creature who kills because of faith.' He would usually wrap up his speeches by pointing to the sky and declaiming theatrically: 'The question of humanity can be solved only by constant dread.' My colleague Abu Salim had a notion that the Professor had links with the terrorist groups because of the violent language he used, but I would loyally defend the man, because they did not understand that he was a philosopher who refused to make foolish jokes, as the stupid ambulance drivers did all day. I remembered every sentence and every word he said, for I was captivated by my affection and admiration for him.

Let me get back to that wretched night. When we turned towards the Martyrs Bridge I noticed that the ambulance driven by Abu Salim had disappeared. Then in the side mirror I caught sight of a police car gaining on us at high speed. I pulled over to the side in the middle of the bridge. Four young men in masks and special police uniforms got out of the police car. The leader of the group pointed his pistol in my face and told me to get out of the vehicle, while his colleagues unloaded the sack of heads from the ambulance.

'I've been kidnapped and they are going to cut off my head.' That was my first thought when they tied me up and stuffed me in the boot of the police car. It took me only 10 minutes to realise what was awaiting me. I recited the Throne Verse from the Quran three times in the darkness of the boot and I felt that my skin was starting to peel off. For some reason in those dark moments I thought about my body weight, maybe 70 kilos. The slower the car went, or the more it turned, the more frightened I was, and when it picked up speed again a strange blend of tranquility and anxiety would pulse through me. Perhaps I thought at those moments of what the Professor had said about the correlation between speed and the imminence of death. I didn't understand exactly what he meant, but he would say that someone about to die in the forest would be more afraid than someone about to die in a speeding ambulance, because the first one feels that fate has singled him out, while the second imagines there are others sticking with him. I also remember that he once announced with a smile: 'I would like to have my death in a spaceship travelling at the speed of light.'

I imagined that all the unidentified and mutilated bodies I had carried in the ambulance since the fall of Baghdad lay before me, and that in the darkness surrounding me I then saw the Professor picking my severed head from a pile of rubbish, while my colleagues made dirty jokes about my liking for the Professor. I don't think the police car drove very far before it came to a halt. At least they did not leave the city. I tried to remember the Rahman Verse of the Quran but they got me out of the car and escorted me into a house which smelt of grilled fish. I could hear a child crying. They undid my blindfold and I found myself in a cold, unfurnished room. Then three madmen laid into me and beat me to a pulp, until a darkness again descended.

I thought I heard a cock crow at first. I shut my eyes but I couldn't sleep. I felt a sharp pain in my left ear. With difficulty I turned over onto my back and pushed myself towards the window, which had recently been blocked up. I was very thirsty. It was easy to work out that I was in a house in one of Baghdad's old neighbourhoods. That was clear from the nature of the walls and particularly the old wooden door. In fact I don't know exactly what details of my story matter to you, for me to get the right of asylum in your country. I find it very hard to describe those days of terror, but I want to mention also some of the things which matter to me. I felt that God, and behind him the Professor, would never abandon me throughout my ordeal. I felt the presence of God intensely in my heart, nurturing my peace of mind and calling me to patience. The Professor kept my mind busy and alleviated the loneliness of my captivity. He was my solace and my comfort.

Throughout those arduous months I would recall what the Professor had said about his friend, Dawoud the engineer. What did he mean by saying that the world is all interconnected? And where do the power and the will of God stand in such matters? We were drinking tea at the hospital door when the Professor said: 'While my friend Dawoud was driving the family car through the streets of Baghdad, an Iraqi poet in London was writing a fiery article in praise of the resistance, with a bottle of whiskey on the table in front of him to help harden his heart. Because the world is all interconnected, through feelings, words, nightmares, and other secret channels, out of the poet's article jumped three masked men. They stopped the family car and killed Dawoud, his wife, his child and his father. His mother was waiting for them at home. Dawoud's mother doesn't know the Iraqi poet nor the masked men. She knows how to cook the fish which was awaiting them. The Iraqi poet fell asleep on the sofa in London in a drunken stupor, while Dawoud's mother's fish went cold and the sun set in Baghdad.'

The wooden door of the room opened and a young man, tall with a pale and haggard face, came in carrying breakfast. He smiled at me as he put the food down in front of me. At first I was uncertain what I could say or do. But then I threw myself at his feet and implored him tearfully: 'I am the father of three children... I'm a religious man who fears God... I have nothing to do with politics or religious denominations... God protect you... I'm just an ambulance driver... before the invasion, and since the invasion... I swear by God and his noble Prophet.' The young man put a finger to his lips and rushed out. I felt that my end had come. I drank the cup of tea and performed my prayers in the hope that God would forgive my sins. At the second prostration I felt that a layer of ice was forming across my body and I almost cried out in fear, but the young man opened the door, carrying a small lighting device attached to a stand, and accompanied by a boy carrying a Kalashnikov rifle. The boy stood next to me, pointing the gun at my head, and from then on he did not leave his place. A fat man in his forties came in, taking no notice of me. On the wall he hung a black cloth banner inscribed with a Quranic verse urging Muslims to fight jihad. Then a masked man came in with a video camera and a small computer. Then a boy came in with a small wooden table. The masked man joked with the boy, tweaked his nose and thanked him, then put the computer on the table and busied himself with setting up the camera in front of the black banner. The thin young man tried out the lighting system three times and then left.

'Abu Jihad, Abu Jihad,' the fat man shouted.

The young man's voice came from outside the room: 'Wait a minute. Right you are, Abu Arkan.'

This time the young man came back carrying the sack of heads which they had taken from the ambulance. Everyone blocked their nose because of the stink from the sack. The fat man asked me to sit in front of the black banner. I felt that my legs were paralysed, but the fat man pulled me roughly by my shirt collar. At that point another man came in, thick-set with one eye, and ordered the fat man to let me be. This man had in his hand an army uniform. The man with one eye sat close to me, with his arm across my shoulders like a friend, and asked me to calm down. He told me they wouldn't slaughter me if I was cooperative and kind-hearted. I didn't understand fully what he meant by this 'kind-hearted'. He told me it would only take a few minutes. The one-eyed man took a small piece of paper from his pocket and asked me to read it. Meanwhile the fat man was taking the decomposing heads out of the sack and lining them up in front of me. It said on the piece of paper that I was an officer in the Iraqi army and these were the heads of other officers, and that accompanied by my fellow officers I had raided houses, raped women and tortured innocent civilians, that we had received orders to kill from a senior officer in the U.S. Army, in return for large financial rewards. The man with one eye asked me to put on the army uniform and the cameraman asked everyone to pull back behind the camera. Then he came up to me and started adjusting my head, as a hairdresser does. After that he adjusted the line of heads, then went back behind the camera and called out: 'Off you go.'

The cameraman's voice was very familiar. Perhaps it resembled the voice of a famous actor, or it might have been like the voice of the Professor when he was making an exaggerated effort to talk softly. After they filmed the videotape, I didn't meet the members of the group again, other than the young man who brought me food, and he prevented me from asking any questions. Every time he brought food he would tell me a new joke about politicians and men of religion. My only wish was that he would let me contact my wife, because I had hidden some money for a rainy day in a place where even the jinn would never think of looking, but they vehemently rejected my request. The one-eyed leader of the group told me that everything depended on the success of the videotape, and in fact the tape was such a success so quickly that everyone was surprised. Al Jazeera broadcast the videotape. They allowed me to watch television and on that day they were jumping for joy, so much so that the fat man kissed me on the head and said I was a great actor. What made me angry was the Al Jazeera newsreader, who assured viewers that the channel had established through reliable sources that the tape was authentic and that the Ministry of Defence had admitted that the officers had gone missing. After the success of the broadcast they started treating me in a manner which was better than good. They took trouble over my food and bedding and allowed me to have a bath. Their kindness culminated on the night they sold me to the second group. Then three masked men from that group came into the room and, after the man with one eye had given me a warm farewell, the new men laid into me with their fists, tied me up and gagged me, then shoved me into the boot of a car which drove off at terrifying speed.

The second group's car travelled far this time. Perhaps we reached the outskirts of Baghdad. They took me out in a desolate village where dogs roamed and barked all over the place. They held me in a cattle pen and there were two men who took turns guarding the pen night and day. I don't know why, but they proceeded to starve me and humiliate me. They were completely different from the first group. They wore their masks all the time and never spoke a word with me. They would communicate with each other through gestures. In fact there was not a human voice to be heard from the village, just the barking of dogs the whole month I spent in the cow pen. The hours passed with oppressive tedium. I would hope that anything would happen, rather than this life sentence with three cows. I gave up thinking about these people, or what religious group or party they belonged to. I no longer bemoaned my fate but felt I had already lived through what happened to me at some time, and that time was a period that would not last long. But my sense of this time made it seem slow and confused. It no longer occurred to me to try to escape or to ask them what they wanted from me. I felt that I was carrying out some mission, a binding duty which I had to perform until my last breath. Perhaps there was a secret power working in league with a human power to play a secret game for purposes too grand for a simple man like me to grasp. 'Every man has both a poetic obligation and a human obligation,' as the Professor used to say. But if that was true, how could I tell the difference, and easily, between the limits of the human obligation and those of the poetic obligation? Because my understanding is that, for example, looking after my wife and children is one of my human obligations, and refusing to hate is a poetic obligation. But why did the Professor say that we confuse the two obligations and do not recognize the diabolical element that drives them both? Because the diabolical obligations imply the capacity to stand in the face of a man when he is pushing his own humanity towards the abyss, and this is too much for the mind of a simple man like me, who barely completed his intermediate education, at least I think so.

What I'm saying has nothing to do with my asylum request. What matters to you is the horror. If the Professor was here, he would say that the horror lies in the simplest of puzzles which shine in a cold star in the sky over this city. In the end they came into the cow pen after midnight one night. One of the masked men spread one corner of the pen with fine carpets. Then his companion hung a black banner inscribed: The Islamic Jihad Group, Iraq Branch. Then the cameraman came in with his camera, and it struck me that he was the same cameraman as the one with the first group. His hand gestures were the same as those of the first cameraman. The only difference was that he was now communicating with the others through gestures alone. They asked me to put on a white dishdasha and sit in front of the black banner. They gave me a piece of paper and told me to read out what was written on it: that I belonged to the Mehdi Army and I was a famous killer, I had cut off the heads of hundreds of Sunni men, and I had support from Iran. Before I'd finished reading, one of the cows gave a loud moo, so the cameraman asked me to read it again. One of the men took the three cows away so that we could finish off the cow pen scene.

I later realised that everyone who bought me was moving me across the same bridge. I don't know why. One group would take me across the Martyrs Bridge towards Karkh on the west bank of the Tigris, then the next group would take me back across the same bridge to Rasafa on the east bank. If I go on like this, I think my story will never end, and I'm worried you'll say what others have said about my story. So I think it would be best if I summarise the story for you, rather than have you accuse me of making it up. They sold me to a third group. The car drove at speed across the Martyrs Bridge once again. I was moved to a luxurious house and this time my prison was a bedroom with a lovely comfortable bed, the kind in which you see film stars having sex. My fear evaporated and I began to grasp the concept of the secret mission for which they had chosen me. I carried out the mission so as not to lose my head, but I also thought I would test their reaction in certain matters. After filming a new video in which I spoke about how I belonged to Sunni Islamist groups and about my work blowing up Shi'ite mosques and public markets, I asked them for some money as payment for making the tape. Their decisive response was a beating I will never forget. Throughout the year and a half of my kidnapping experience, I was moved from one hiding place to another. They shot video of me talking about how I was a treacherous Kurd, an infidel Christian, a Saudi terrorist, a Syrian Baathist intelligence agent, or a Revolutionary Guard from Zoroastrian Iran. On these videotapes I murdered, raped, started fires, planted bombs and carried out crimes that no sane person would even imagine. All these tapes were broadcast on satellite channels around the world. Experts, journalists and politicians sat there discussing what I said and did. The only bad luck we ran into was when we made a video in which I appeared as a Spanish soldier, with a resistance fighter holding a knife to my neck, demanding Spanish forces withdraw from Iraq. All the satellite stations refused to broadcast the tape because Spanish forces had left the country a year earlier. I almost paid a heavy price for this mistake when the group holding me wanted to kill me in revenge for what had happened, but the cameraman saved me by suggesting another wonderful idea, the last of my videotape roles. They dressed me in the costume of an Afghan fighter, trimmed my beard and put a black turban on my head. Five men stood behind me and they brought in six men screaming and crying out for help from God, his Prophet and the Prophet's family. They slaughtered the men in front of me like sheep as I announced that I was the new leader of the al Qaida organization in Mesopotamia and made threats against everyone in creation.

Late one night the cameraman brought me my old clothes and took me to the ambulance, which was standing at the door. They put those six heads in a sack and threw it into the vehicle. At that moment I noticed the cameraman's gestures and I thought that surely he was the cameraman for all the groups and maybe the mastermind of this dreadful game. I sat behind the steering wheel with trembling hands. Then the cameraman gave the order from behind his mask: 'You know the way. Cross the Martyrs Bridge, to the hospital.'

I am asking for asylum in your country because of everyone. They are all killers and schemers – my wife, my children, my neighbours, my colleagues, God, his Prophet, the government, the newspapers, even the Professor whom I thought an angel, and now I have suspicions that the cameraman with the terrorist groups was the Professor himself. His enigmatic language was merely proof of his connivance and his vile nature. They all told me I hadn't been away for a year and half, because I came back the morning after working that rainy night, and on that very morning the Professor said to me: 'The world is just a bloody and hypothetical story, and we are all killers and heroes.' And those six heads cannot be proof of what I'm saying, just as they are not proof that the night will not spread across the sky.

Three days after this story was filed away in the records of the immigration department, they took the man who told it to the psychiatric hospital. Before the doctor could start asking him about his childhood memories, the ambulance driver summed up his real story in four words: 'I want to sleep.'

It was a humble entreaty.

An Army Newspaper

To the Dead of the Iran-Iraq War (1980-88)

WE WILL GO to the cemetery, to the mortuary, and ask the guardians of the past for permission. We'll take the dead man out to the public garden naked and set him on the platform under the ripe orange sun. We'll try to hold his head in place. An insect, a fly buzzes around him, although flies buzz equally around the living and the dead. We'll implore him to repeat the story to us. There's no need to kick him in the balls for him to tell the story honestly and impartially, because the dead are usually honest, even the bastards among them.

★

Thank you, dear writer, for brushing the fly from my nose and giving me this golden opportunity. I disagree with you only when you try to make the readers frightened of me by describing me as a bastard. Let them judge for themselves, I beg you, and don't you too turn into a rabid dog. Congratulations on being alive! Just don't interfere with the nature of the animal that you are.

Your Honour, ten years ago, that is before I ended my life, I was working for an army newspaper, supervising the cultural page which dealt with war stories and poems. I lived a safe life. I had a young son and a faithful wife who cooked well and had recently agreed to suck my cock every time we had sex. From my work at the newspaper I received many rewards and presents, worth much more than my monthly salary. As the editor will attest, I was the only genius able to enliven the cultural page through my indefatigable imagination in the art of combat. So much so that even the minister of culture himself commended me, gave me his special patronage and promised me in secret that he would get rid of the editor and appoint me in his place. I was not a genius to that extent, nor was I a bastard as the writer of this story wants to portray me. I was a diligent and ambitious man who dreamt of becoming minister of culture and nothing more. To that end I was dedicated in those days to doing my job with honour, as with the sweat of my brow I revised, designed and perfected my cultural page like a patient baker. No, Your Honour, I was not a censor, as you imagine, because the soldiers who wrote were stricter and more disciplined than any censor I ever met in my life. They would scrutinise every word and examine each letter with a magnifying glass. They were not so stupid as to send in pieces that were plaintive, or full of whining and screaming. Some of them wrote because it helped them believe that they would not be killed and that the war was just an upbeat story in a newspaper. Others were seeking some financial or other benefits. There were writers who were forced to write, but all that doesn't interest me now because at this stage I have no regrets and I am not even afraid. The dead, Your Honour, do not agonise over their crimes and do not long to be happy, as you know. If from time to time we hear the opposite, then those are just trivial religious and poetical exaggerations and ridiculous rumours which have nothing to do with the real circumstances of the simple dead.

But I do admit that I would often interfere in the structure and composition of the stories and poems, and try as far as possible to add imaginative touches to the written images which would come to us from the front. For God's sake, what's the point, as we are about to embark on war in poetry, of someone saying: 'I felt that the artillery bombardment was as hard as rain, but we were not afraid'? I would cross that out and rewrite it: 'I felt that the artillery fire was like a carnival of stars, as we staggered like lovers across the soil of the homeland.' This is just a small example of my modest interventions.

But the turning point in the story, Your Honour, came when five stories arrived at the newspaper from a soldier who said he had written them in one month. Each story was written in a thick exercise book of the coloured kind used in schools. On the cover of each exercise book the writer had filled in the boxes for name, class and school, and none of the classes went beyond the primary level and each book bore a different name. Each of the stories was about a soldier with the same name as the name written on the cover. The stories were written in a surprisingly elevated literary style. In fact I swear that the world's finest novels, before these stories that I read, were mere drivel, vacuous stories eclipsed by the grandeur of what this soldier had written. The stories did not speak of the war, though the heroes of them were all reluctant soldiers. They were a transparent and cruel exploration of sexual beings from a point of view that was childlike and satanic at the same time. One would read about soldiers in full battle dress, cavorting and laughing with their lovers in gardens and on the banks of rivers, about soldiers who transformed the thighs of prostitutes into marble arches entwined with sad plants the colour of milk, soldiers who described the sky in short lascivious sentences as they rested their heads on the breasts of lissom women; magical anthems about bodies that secreted water lilies.

Quickly and with fascination I made inquiries to find out on which front and with which military unit the author of these stories was fighting. I discovered that a few days before the stories were sent, the enemy had made a devastating attack on the army corps with which he was fighting, and the corps had suffered appalling losses in lives and equipment. I had a colleague who worked as an editor on the bravery and medals page in our newspaper and who would shout out whenever he saw me: 'You have the brain of a tank, comrade!' I remembered this description of his when I felt the idea flash fully formed in the golden wires of my brain, as I skimmed through these miraculous exercise books. I decided to write the soldier a threatening letter, telling him firmly and frankly that he was liable to interrogation by the Baath Party, and perhaps would soon be tried and executed, because his stories were a deliberate and manifest deviation from the party's programme in the just war. I relied on the perpetual fear of a soldier, which is widely acknowledged, to persuade him to renounce these stories or apologise to me and beg me bitterly to destroy what he had written, or to forgive him his atrocious act, which he would never repeat. Only then would I know what to do with these sublime stories of humanity. I doubt any great novelist could dream of writing more than five stories displaying such a high level of inventiveness, combining reality and the language of dreams to attain the tenth rank of language, the rank from which fire is created, and from which, in turn, devils are spawned.

Heaven was not far off. It came to my side with lightning speed. One week after my letter to the soldier I received a message from his army corps to say that the soldier had been killed in the latest attack and that no one in his detachment had come out alive. I almost wept for joy at the bounteous gift that destiny had brought as, indescribably elated, I read again the name of the dead soldier.

Your Honour, five months after publishing the first story in my own name (after inventing a distinctive title), I was travelling the countries of the world to present my new story at seminars where the most famous critics and intellectuals would introduce me. The biggest newspapers and international literary magazines wrote about me. I could not even find enough time to give television and radio interviews. The local critics wrote long studies on how our just war could inspire in man such artistic largesse, such love, such poetry. Many master's and doctoral theses were written in the nation's universities and in them the researchers endeavoured to explore all the insights into poetry and humanity in my story. They wrote about the harmonies between bullets and fate, between the sound of planes and the rocking of a bed, between the kiss and the piece of shrapnel, between the smell of gunpowder and the smell of a woman's vulva, although the story did not make the slightest mention of war, directly or indirectly. When I came home, at a lavish ceremony I was awarded the post of minister of culture with no trouble at all. I was in no hurry to publish the four remaining stories, because the first story still had more to yield. I changed my wife, my house, my clothes and my car for new things that I coveted. I can say that I paid homage to the war and raised my hands to heaven in gratitude for the bounty and the priceless gifts. I was confident that the Nobel Prize for Literature would be here on my desk in the ministry after the fifth story. The gates of happiness had opened, as they say.

Then one day three large parcels from the front arrived at my address at the ministry, containing twenty stories sent it seemed by the same soldier in the same manner: primary school books bearing the names of soldiers, containing tales of love and destiny. At first I felt tremendous confusion, which soon turned into icy panic. I quickly picked up the stories and asked the man in charge of the ministry stores to give me the keys to one of the storerooms. I hid them in complete secrecy and made many and intensive contacts to find the soldier. All the messages would come directly to my office in the ministry, and all of them confirmed that the soldier had been killed. They were frightening days. On the following day other parcels arrived, with double the number of stories this time, from the same soldier and in the same manner. Again I carried the stories to the storeroom and put extra padlocks on the door. Cruel months passed, Your Honour, with me torn between hiding the stories which continued to flood in at an amazing rate and looking for the soldier, of whom there was no trace the length and breadth of the front. In the meantime the second story had been printed and released. I received phone calls from the president, the minister of defence and other state officials, lauding my loyalty and my genius. Invitations from abroad began to flood into the ministry, but this time I turned them all down on the grounds that the country was more precious and more important than all the prizes and conferences in the world, and the country needed all its righteous citizens in such trying circumstances. In fact I wanted to find a solution to the problem of the stories, which kept arriving every morning in vast numbers, like a storm of locusts: today a hundred stories, tomorrow two hundred and so on.

Your Honour, I almost lost my 'tank brain'. At last I obtained the address of the soldier's house and went to visit his family to make sure he was dead. His mother told me she did not believe he was dead. There was only a small hole in his forehead. It was a sniper's bullet. I took the address of his grave from his wife and left them some money. The other storerooms at the ministry were crammed with exercise books. How would I explain to the party and the government that I had written all these stories, and why was I writing them in exercise books, and why the names of the soldiers, seemingly in primary school. And why was I storing them this way? There were dozens of questions, none of which had a logical answer.

I bought some old flour warehouses on the edge of the city in case more stories poured in. I paid vast amounts to three workers in the ministry to help dig up the soldier's grave. There he was with his decayed body and a hole in his forehead. I shook his body several times to make sure he was dead. I whispered in his ear, then shouted and insulted him. I challenged him, if he could, to open his mouth or move his little finger. But he was dead enough. A worm came out of his neck chasing another worm, then the two of them disappeared inside again somewhere near his shoulder.

Your Honour, you may not believe this story but I swear by your omnipotence that within a year the flour warehouses and the ministry storerooms were crammed with the soldier's stories. Of course I didn't have a chance to read all the stories, but I would take a sample of each batch and I swear to you that they did not increase only in number, they also became increasingly brilliant and creative. But at the time I trembled and felt that my end would come soon if this flood of stories did not cease. Certainly I left no stone unturned in my inquiries and research. I looked into the addresses from which the parcels were coming. They were being sent in the name of the soldier from various parts of the front but there was no trace of him. Nevertheless I could not go too far in asking about the parcels for fear of being exposed.

I went back to the grave and burnt the soldier's body. I divorced my second wife and left my job after a psychiatrist helped me by submitting a report saying that my health was deteriorating. I collected all the exercise books from the ministry storerooms and the old flour warehouses and bought some isolated agricultural land where I built a special incinerator, a large storeroom, a room and a toilet, and surrounded it with a high wall. I was sure that the stories would keep pouring in at this new address, but I was prepared for them this time. As I expected, from the morning of the first day at the farm I was working hard day and night, burning the coloured exercise books – all the stories, and all the soldier's names – in the hope that the war would end and that this madness of khaki sperm would also stop.

The war did stop, Your Honour, after long and terrifying years, but a new war broke out. The only option left to me was the incinerator fire, as you are the Merciful, the Forgiving.

Your Honour...

So now, and before I'm put back in the mortuary, I know you are the Omnipotent, the Wise, the Omniscient and the Imperious, but did you also once work for an army newspaper? And why do you need an incinerator for your characters?

The Composer

JAAFAR AL-MUTALLIBI WAS born in the town of al-Amara. In 1973 he resigned from the Communist Party and joined the ruling Baath Party. In the same year his wife gave birth to their second son. Jaafar was a professional lute-player and a renowned composer of patriotic songs. He was killed in the uprising in the city of Kirkuk in 1991.

Today I can tell you about how he died. Do you see this old woman shouting out the price of fish? She's my mother. We've been selling fish since we came back to Baghdad. Let me help her empty the crate of fish, then let's go to a nearby coffee shop and talk:

After the end of the war between Iraq and Iran my father started to proclaim his atheism blatantly and caused us many problems. One evening he came home with his shirt stained with blood. It seems he'd had a nosebleed after one of his friends punched him. They were playing dominoes in the coffee shop when my father launched into a tirade of obscene insults to God and the Prophet. He made them up and set them to music during the game. As you know, he was a well-known composer. At first my father whistled a tune composed in the military style, then he added a new insult: a nail in the testicle of God's sister!

Many people burst out laughing when they heard the insults which my father's imagination came up with, but they soon began to keep away from him and ask God for forgiveness. Some of them avoided meeting him in the street.

One of them told him in jest one day that he hoped a truck loaded with steel would run him over, but everyone was frightened of his connection with the government. The day after he was punched he wrote a report for party headquarters about Abu Alaa, the man who hit him, and two days later Abu Alaa disappeared. We were living in a neighbourhood called the Second Qadissiya, which consisted of houses the government had assigned to junior army officers, other people who had moved from cities in the south and centre of the country and the families of Kurds who worked for the regime. We were the only family in the neighbourhood that earned its living differently. All the families except us lived off salaries from the army, the party and the security services, while we lived off the patriotic songs that my father composed. My father had a status higher than that of the mayor and members of the local hierarchy of the party, because the president himself had more than once awarded him military medals for his songs about the war, songs which people remember to this day.

Listen, brother, I'll sum up the story for you. One year after the war ended, my father suffered what the newspapers call writer's block and he was unable to compose new music for the many poems celebrating the greatness of the president which famous poets would send him. Months passed, then a year, and he still could not write a single new tune. Do you know what he did in the meantime? He took it upon himself to write and set to music short depraved poems making fun of religion. One warm winter's evening we were watching television when we heard my father singing a new song of his about the Prophet's wives and how loose they were. Suddenly my elder brother sprang up, took my father's pistol from the wardrobe, jumped on top of my father and put the pistol in his mouth. He would have killed him were it not for my mother, who tore open her dress, baring her breasts and screaming. My brother was transfixed for a moment as he looked at my mother's enormous breasts, which hung down over her stomach like an animal whose guts had spilled out. This was the first time we had ever seen my mother's breasts, except as babies. I went into the bathroom and my brother fled the sight of my mother by leaving the house. She was illiterate but she was smarter than my father, whom she looked after in a curious way. She spoilt him as if he were a son. She was the licensed midwife in the Qadissiya district and people were very fond of her. My father decided to submit a report on my brother to the local party headquarters but they did not react to it. My father's name had started to stink in the neighbourhood and in artistic circles. They said that Jaafar al-Mutallibi had gone mad, and his old friends avoided him. He travelled to Baghdad and submitted a request to the radio and television station asking them to rebroadcast the war songs he had composed, or at least one song a week. They rejected his request and told him his songs were now inappropriate. They were only broadcasting patriotic songs twice a year: on the anniversary of the outbreak of the war and the anniversary of when it ended. My father wanted to restore his past and his fame by any means possible. He tried but failed to meet the president. He submitted an application to the film and theatre department, proposing a documentary film about his songs and his music but that request was also ignored. While he was making all these attempts he finished composing the music to ten songs insulting God and existence, as well as a beautiful song about the first four caliphs. We realised he had gone completely mad when he started frequenting the studios and trying to persuade them to record him singing his songs making fun of religion. Of course his requests were rejected categorically, and some people threw him out and threatened to kill him. In the end my father decided to record his songs on tape at home. He sat in front of a tape recorder and started to sing and play the lute. Of course it was a poor recording but it was intelligible. He played it to us at breakfast and we were worried that people would find out about this tape. We tried to get hold of it and destroy it but he would never let it leave his coat pocket and when he went to sleep he would slip it into a special pocket he made in the pillow.

Today there's no need to hide this copy because others need it, and religion has made more progress than necessary, along with the murderers and thieves. The reaction of the street might be hysterical, but let's fire a bullet in the air. Go ahead, you're a journalist, it will be good for you and good for everyone. A young singer offered to sing it and record it again in a modern studio but I refused. These songs must remain as my father himself recorded them, as evidence of his story. They can only be copied. People soon forget the stories of this event. When you tell them these stories, after a time they think the stories are figments of imagination. Take our neighbour in the market, for example, Abu Sadiq who sells onions. When he now tells his story about the battle with the Iranians at the River Jassim, it sounds like a Hollywood horror story he made up.

The government army ran away and the Kurdish Peshmerga militias entered Kirkuk. The people of the city welcomed the uprising with great joy. There was overwhelming chaos, gunfire, dead bodies, Kurdish dancing and songs everywhere. We were unable to escape. The insurgents set fire to houses in all the government districts and where party members lived. They killed and strung up the bodies of the Baathists, police and security people. We were holed up at home and a group of young men broke down the reinforced door to my father's office. They took us out on the street to carry out the death sentence on us. My mother was on her knees pleading with them but she did not rip her clothes this time. What? My father? No, no, my father wasn't with us. Months before the uprising, he had become the madman of the city, wandering the streets singing against God and carrying his lute, which no longer had a single string. A fire broke out in our house and my mother collapsed unconscious as the rest of us leant against the outer wall of the house.

Umm Tariq, our Kurdish neighbour, turned up at the last moment, screaming at the young men and speaking to them in their language. Then she started imploring them to set us free. She told them how kind and generous my mother was and how she helped the Kurdish women give birth and looked after pregnant women. She told them how my mother would give away bread to the neighbours in honour of Abbas, the son of the Imam Ali at feast time, and how brave my elder brother was and how he'd been best friends with her son who'd been killed fighting with the Peshmerga forces during the Anfal campaign, and that it was he who helped her late son escape from Kirkuk (here she lied), and that I was a good peaceful boy who wouldn't hurt a fly. She ended her defence of us on an angry note. 'They're not responsible for what that pimp Jaafar al-Mutallibi has been doing,' she said. Then she spat on the ground. We went into Umm Tariq's house and we didn't leave until the Republican Guard forces entered the city and the Peshmerga militias withdrew. Most of the insurgents ran away with the militias.

In the end we found my father without a head, tied to a farm tractor with a thick rope. He had been dragged around the city streets for a whole day and his corpse had been put on display in a manner that is impossible to imagine. At the time they were about to execute us my father was close to the local party headquarters, where the bodies of the party members filled the courtyard. My father went into the empty building and headed for the information room. My father knew this room well because it was from this room that his patriotic songs used to be broadcast from loudspeakers on the roof during the first war. From the same loudspeakers the party members would also speak to the public when someone was being executed for deserting the army or for helping the Peshmerga militias. My father put the tape into the tape player and the loudspeakers started broadcasting to the insurgents his songs attacking God and existence. My father was hugging his lute and smiling when the insurgents arrived.

HASSAN BLASIM

They took him outside. Excuse me, my friend. There's a fish dealer who's bringing some sacks of carp, so I have to go now. Tomorrow I'll tell you the secret of my father's relationship with Umm Tariq, the Kurdish woman.

The Virgin and the Soldier

A WHISKEY BOTTLE had been forced up the corpse's arse, three fingers had been cut off his right hand and there were other horrible injuries, as if it were the work of wolves rather than humans. It was the body of a man in his mid-thirties. He wasn't one of the victims of the sectarian killing which intensified in Baghdad in 2006, although the body did show up at that time. Perhaps someone had shoved the whiskey bottle in with their foot. Perhaps it had been carefully inserted there. The man was not a policeman, or a translator working treacherously with the U.S. Army, not a journalist or a militia leader, not even a random civilian. He was just a man who fell victim to a macabre story. The body belonged to a man called Hamid al-Sayid, who had been released when the government emptied most of the prisons of inmates shortly before the fall of Baghdad in 2003.

Hamid al-Sayid would have been well-known if the newspapers ten years earlier had written about what happened in the the army uniform factory which belonged to the Military Industrialisation Organisation. But at the time all the parties involved had covered up what happened, and of course every party had its reasons. The Saddam Hussein regime took the view that all events unrelated to major national issues were mere details devoid of meaning or importance, and that it was unwise to let the people take an interest in matters which would distract them from the real battle against the iniquitous forces of imperialism and Zionism, especially at a time when Iraq faced the relentless economic blockade imposed by the United Nations after the first Gulf War. As for Hamid's family, they had hushed the matter up, firstly out of fear and secondly out of embarrassment. The rest of the wolves had been tracking Hamid down for the past ten years, and when Hamid's elder sister saw his body she knew at once who had killed her younger brother, because the three severed fingers were a clue to the identity of the perpetrator.

The story began in 1996, in the Karama factory for sewing military uniforms, when U.N. inspectors found Hamid and a dead girl in one of the rooms at the factory. Or rather it began on the last day before the factory's ill-fated holiday break. Maybe God intervened directly in the events of that day, maybe what happened was the work of devils from the kingdom of chance, or perhaps everything was part of the dirty deeds of man.

It was a small and friendly gesture but very cautious, the way Fatin winked at the soldier who passed by nervously carrying a pile of papers. Then Fatin bent down over the sewing machine again to stitch the army badge in the shape of a red triangle onto the soldier's trouser pocket. After a while Hamid al-Sayid retraced his steps, crossing the sewing room from the middle towards the small iron staircase that led to the second floor. But this time he did not receive another wink from Fatin, because everyone's eyes were like security cameras. In a factory like this one mistake could cost dear. This was Hamid al-Sayid's little war. In his room he would examine the factory accounts and listen to the whir of the needles in the sewing machines. He liked Fatin or, as he told his dear sister Sahira, was madly in love with her, but so far he had not found a way to meet Fatin outside the factory. Hamid lived on the Rusafa side of Baghdad in the Shaab district while Fatin lived far away in the Police district with her three brothers and their wives. She was maybe twenty-two years old. I'm not sure if she was the only unmarried woman in the Karama factory. Zainab says that maybe there were five of them in the factory. By the way, the manager of the factory had suggested changing its name to the Leader factory for Sewing Military Uniforms, and had written an official application to that effect to the Military Industrialisation Organisation. The Karama factory was going to have a fifteen-day holiday starting the next day. They told them this holiday was a bonus granted by his Excellency, the Minister. As far as Hamid was concerned the days of this wretched holiday were going to feel like a century. In her messages Fatin was always reminding him of her brothers, whenever Hamid tried to persuade her to fix a time for a meeting outside the factory walls. 'Hamid, if my brothers found out they would slaughter me like a chicken. You're crazy. I don't even go to the door of the house,' she would say. Hamid did not know how he would survive the holiday break without Fatin's smile, which he took home with him every day to contemplate for hours, and kissed before he went to sleep.

That day the factory manager summoned Abu Fadil the gatekeeper by telephone. Abu Fadil hurriedly wrapped up the newspaper from which he was eating aubergine and onions and wiped his mouth with his hand. This man was in his late fifties and so frighteningly thin he looked like he had just emerged from the grave. He held the first of the keys which would become the focus of suspicion. No one had ever seen Abu Fadil wear any trousers other than his one grey pair, and his baggy grey suit was as sad as the doors in the old district. Abu Fadil remembered the names of all the women who sewed, which was truly a remarkable achievement. It was easy to remember the names of the soldiers because there were only seven of them in the factory. Apart from Colonel Zahran the manager and Abu Fadil the gatekeeper, there was Hamid and Rahman in the accounts and auditing room, Sadiq and Omar, who were in charge of supervising the trucks which picked up the uniforms from the back door of the factory, then Sergeant Jassim Khodeir and his assistants, Khalaf and Marwan. The sergeant was in charge of maintaining the sewing machines. The other factory affairs were managed by women workers. But Colonel Zahran was the only man in the factory who could observe the sewing women all the time. He sat in a room with glass walls directly facing the room where the women worked on the ground floor. On the second floor there was the accounts room and three small rooms for sewing supplies, next to the staircase which went down to the ground floor. It was a very small factory but busy, specialising in making uniforms only for senior officers. Today it is rubble because U.S. planes bombed it before Baghdad was occupied.

In the colonel's room, Abu Fadil climbed up on a chair to take down the picture of the president hanging on the wall behind the colonel's desk. The colonel gave him a new picture of the president. In the old picture the president was wearing Arab dress and in the new picture military uniform. The colonel thanked Abu Fadil, then took a bunch of keys from one of the drawers in his desk. He picked out a small key and gave it to Abu Fadil, who added it to his chain of keys, bowing respectfully to the colonel before leaving. If we went out now to the sewing room, we would see the 'second key', that is Sabria, who is in charge of monitoring the work of the women who do the sewing. Sabria circulates constantly between the sewing machines, playing with her bunch of keys and watching everything that happens in the factory. Nobody can stand this Sabria, who is a spinster and a bitch, at least that's what the girls call the woman in charge of monitoring them. Were it not for Sabria's long black hair, there would be nothing to show that she is a woman. That's what Private Rahman says, and he is quite right, because this woman looks like a heavyweight wrestler. By the way, Sabrina is among the few who do not cover their hair in the factory, while most girls wear hijabs with their dark blue factory uniforms. Sabria is from the 1970s generation, which has not yet adapted to the hijab custom and to the rising trend for religious extremism. But she is disgustingly jealous and envious. With the eye of a hawk she monitors every movement, every laugh and every whisper that emanates from the girls.

On the second floor we find the 'third key', that is Private Rahman, but we cannot work out exactly what he is. Maybe he is just a 'personal key'. Private Rahman is Hamid al-Sayid's colleague in the accounts room and Hamid is afraid of Rahman's tongue in case he lets slip a word about his relationship with Fatin. Hamid has little fear of prison but what makes him anxious is the fear that his reputation might be tarnished in the eyes of the manager, Colonel Zahran, who considers Hamid to be the model of an upright soldier and a righteous man. Colonel Zahran has advised Hamid to think seriously about getting married, or 'completing his religion' as they say. He has also urged him to start performing his prayers immediately and repent to God, because this world is transient. Hamid ensures his colleague's silence by ignoring Rahman's habit of going to the men's toilets every half an hour. Rahman takes advantage of the fact that the toilets are on the ground floor near the staircase, with the women's toilets on the right of the staircase and the men's on the left. Rahman feasts his eyes for a moment on the faces of the sewing girls and breathes in the smell that drifts across from the sweat of the girls' bodies, as though it were the smell of paradise. Rahman goes into the toilets to perform each time the same puzzling ritual: he looks in his pockets, takes a box of matches out of the back pocket of his trousers as he holds a cigarette in his lips. Out of another pocket he extracts a picture, dropping a small key in the meantime. He picks up the key and lights his cigarette. It's a picture of a well-known Turkish actress, naked. Rahman starts to make imaginary love to her, pursing his lips as he gazes at the Turkish woman's asshole until his semen gushes out on his hand.

Zainab Mansour runs her hand up and down the zipper of the military trousers like a man masturbating, then kicks the seat of the trousers aside with a theatrical gesture, making the sewing women burst into laughter. Zainab holds the fourth key and has freedom of movement around the factory by virtue of her work as assistant to Sabria the spinster. Zainab is the best friend of Rahman's elder sister Sahira and at work she acts as messenger between Fatin and Hamid. She carries written messages when she goes up to the second floor to fetch sewing supplies. She is a cheerful and intelligent girl and some of the girls think she's a lesbian. That day Zainab had a long laugh when she heard Sergeant Khodeir talking seriously about sewing machine breakdowns as though he were a professor of biology. Quietly and confidently, and with some irritation, he says: 'The needle can break more than once during stitching for several reasons: the presser foot may not be properly in place, the bobbin may be inserted incorrectly, or the material may be being pulled too forcefully. If the thread breaks at the needle, then the thread is not feeding properly or the tension of the thread is wrong. If the teeth of the comb are worn or dirty, the stitching will not be even. Although the sewing women are professionals, they often make elementary mistakes in sewing.' Zainab listens to him with amusement and he slips her three keys without pausing in his explanation. She puts them in the pocket of her factory uniform as the conversation continues.

There may be other keys but I have chosen just these keys because of the rhythm of the story which Zainab was telling.

On the morning of the first day of the holiday at the Karama factory, an American spy satellite was orbiting in outer space taking pictures in various formats of the little factory, which was troubling the U.N. committee of inspectors set up to look for internationally prohibited weapons. The government was intent on misleading the inspectors and would not allow them to visit the factory more than once. In reality there was nothing in the factory but army uniforms, but the government's aim was to make the U.N. inspectors suspect that the factory was used for prohibited military purposes. The location of the factory, on the edges of Baghdad on barren and abandoned land, helped add to the suspicions. Perhaps the factory had been used in the past for secret military purposes, since its original design did not suggest that it was built as a sewing factory, and the thick steel doors on the second-floor rooms – small rooms without windows – also raised doubts. From the floor tiles in the sewing room, it looked like the place had been used as a laboratory and as a place where water was often used. The paved road nearest the factory was three miles away, and there were two main gates, one at the back used by trucks, and the front gate for the workers to come in and out, where there was a guard post for Abu Fadil the gatekeeper, who would lock the gate after work.

On that morning the American satellite pictures could not of course detect the muffled screams on the second floor. The screaming was hardly audible, and desperate. From the end of a world that was dying it reached the sewing room, which was empty and looked like a dreary sunset over an abandoned city. Fatin screamed and sobbed throughout the night like a slaughtered animal. She wept and raised hell with her screams in the sewing supplies room, while Private Hamid sat in the corner of the room trying to control his hands, which were trembling like a branch in a storm.

My aunt Zainab also wept bitterly whenever she retold the story of what happened on that day. She accused everyone, then she would ask her Lord to forgive her her suspicions. My aunt would say: 'We had finished work and the girls in the room were changing their clothes. Some of the girls changed their clothes and left quickly. In the last hour of work I had given Fatin Hamid's message, in which he begged her if they could talk a moment on the second floor, to take advantage of the time set aside for changing. Fatin had made the excuse that she had to go to the women's toilets because she had diarrhoea. I thought that Hamid would talk to her for a few minutes. Fatin had to catch one of the buses which take us into town. It's true that on that day people were yelling, joking and laughing in the buses because of the unexpected holiday. But why didn't Fatin's colleagues notice she was missing? God alone knows. I told you I was on another bus. Do you think it was Rahman who committed this crime? No, no, it's impossible Rahman would do such a thing, he's too much of a coward. What if the colonel himself wanted to take revenge on the two of them? Abu Fadil said he didn't lock the second-floor rooms because of the holiday, and Sabria confirmed that. Because the rooms for sewing supplies were usually left open. And then the holiday was only fifteen days. Why, my Lord, why didn't the inspectors come on the second or the third day? What bad luck she had, dear Fatin! The inspectors went into the factory two weeks after the holiday began. Such a world is impossible to understand, and people are frightening.'

'Why didn't you tell them the truth?'

'What truth?'

'The question of the message. One of them might have guessed that Fatin and Hamid were in the factory.'

'When Fatin's three brothers came to our house and spoke to my husband, I told them all about the affair between Fatin and Hamid. Everyone thought that Hamid and Fatin had run off to another town. There was even a rumour they had eloped abroad.'

*

Hamid was holding Fatin's hand as she leant against the wall, trying to persuade her to set a time to meet during the holiday. They could hear the girls' voices from the changing room. Hamid opened the door of the third sewing supplies room, pulled Fatin inside and then closed the door behind him. In the middle of the room there was a large heap of army uniforms which were unfit for use because of faults in the design. The only other things in the room were boxes containing sewing supplies, such as thread, large scissors for cutting cloth and other small things. Hamid began to kiss her passionately all over her face. Fatin yielded to the pleasure of his kisses and tried to suppress her sighs. Then she heard the sound of footsteps approaching the door to the room.

Private Hamid tells the judge in the court martial that he heard the footsteps of someone coming along the corridor, and that he and Fatin hid under the heap of army uniforms. Then they heard him stop at the door, open the door a little, reach inside with his arm without coming into the room, switch the light on and then turn it off again.

'Did you see the person's arm? Was it the arm of a man?'

'No, I didn't see his arm.'

'How do you know he didn't come into the room?'

'I judged that by the light coming from the corridor.'

'What happened after that?'

'He turned the key in the lock and left.'

'Now tell me in the Lord's name, if you have a Lord, didn't you rape her?'

'I swear by almighty God that I didn't rape her. By the third day we were dying of thirst and I lost hope that I could break down the door. She told me that getting out would be much the same as dying inside the room. Either way we would be killed. Then she asked me to make love.'

'Did you know she was a virgin?'

'Yes, I knew.'

'Listen, you're an evil man, a rapist, a dog and a son of a whore, and you should have died of hunger and thirst there in the room. But evil men like you are lucky. I could shoot you in the head now with impunity. You lived on the flesh and blood of a dead person. Was she still alive when you committed your second revolting crime?'

'I swear, Your Honour, I wasn't fully conscious. Seven days had passed with us trapped in the room and Fatin was stretched out dead in the middle of the room.'

'But the doctor's reports say she wasn't dead when you cut off her fingers.'

'I swear she was dead. At the time I didn't have the strength to open my eyes I was so weak and hungry and thirsty. I tried to drink a little urine but...'

'But what? You drank her blood. Let's assume you're a man of flesh and blood. Well, why did you eat three of her fingers? God forgive you. For example, why didn't you eat any other part of her body?'

'I thought that perhaps dead people feel pain too and the fingers would hurt less.'

'Hamid al-Sayid, did you cut three fingers off the hand of Fatin Qasim?'

'Yes, Your Honour.'

'Did you cut the three fingers with cloth scissors?'

'Yes, Your Honour.'

'Did you eat the three fingers?'

'Yes, Your Honour, I ate them.'

The Madman of Freedom Square

IN THOSE UNFORGETTABLE days before the miracle happened and I discovered the truth which everyone now denies or ignores, we used to guard the platform where the two statues stood. We had light arms, three mortars and seven RPG launchers. The prominent people and opinion-makers in the neighbourhood had rejected an order from the new government to remove the statues and we had information that the army would storm the neighbourhood by night. While I didn't, deep down, consider this to be my battle, it was much easier to deceive myself than to bear the shame of running away. The battle might break out at any moment and I might lose my life for the sake of these two young men cut from stone who stood upright on the dais as though they were about to fall flat on their faces. It's clear that the sculptor was just a building worker who knew nothing of the art of sculpture. The fanatical Islamists had a fatwa that all the statues in the country should be removed because they were idols and incompatible with Islamic law. As for the government, it had decided to remove everything that symbolised the period of the former dictatorial regime. The notables and other people of the neighbourhood held the view that the statues had nothing to do with the former regime nor with repressive fatwas. I didn't believe in that kind of nonsense. My father said it was a symbolic battle of destiny for the sake of the neighbourhood's future. I don't know how my father, as a science teacher in the secondary school, could believe such superstitions. Of course there are dozens of versions of the statues story but perhaps the version that my grandfather told was the one closest to the truth. The touch of realism in my grandfather's story made the people of the neighbourhood seem even more naïve, whereas his intention was to portray them as friendly, intelligent and generous. This is what I was thinking at the time, before my life changed for ever.

Perhaps it would be best if I first repeated to you in brief my grandfather's version of the story, before I tell you what happened to me on the night of the battle. With great sadness he would say: 'No one knows when exactly the two young men appeared. They were the same age, the same height and as alike as twins. People in the neighbourhood thought they were from those rich districts far away but they could not guess where they were going. Each of them carried a backpack and they wore smart clothes suggesting they were wealthy and well-bred. What struck the people of the neighbourhood most was their blond hair and their white complexions. The Darkness district was one of the most wretched in the city and the inhabitants were skinny with swarthy complexions they had inherited from their peasant ancestors. It was the people in nearby parts of the city who gave the name Darkness to the neighbourhood, the only one that did not have electricity. I imagine it was the first time the people of the neighbourhood had seen visitors of this species of humanity.

Every morning the two young men would walk through the village towards the river in the distance, coming from the direction of the wasteland that separates the Darkness district from the Arbanjiya district. They would smile tenderly and with affection at the half-naked children of the neighbourhood, and greet the elders with a slight nod which suggested respect. They would avoid the muddy patches in the lanes simply and unassumingly, without showing signs of disgust or haughtiness. The people of the neighbourhood saw them as angels from heaven. Nobody spoke to them or asked them any intrusive questions, or stood in their way for any reason whatsoever. The neighbourhood was dazzled by the aura of light which radiated from the young men. They would walk with confident, measured steps, as though they had learnt to walk in a private school. Their silence added to the mystery of them. They were well-mannered and dignified, but with a light touch of good humour. The people of the neighbourhood fell in love with the two young men and grew accustomed to their radiant appearance every morning. Day by day people became more and more attached to the two handsome youths, and their coming and going became like the rising and the setting of the sun. The children were the first to grow attached to them: they would gather early in the morning on the edge of the quarter to wait for the young men to appear from across the wasteland. They would bet Sinbad cards on which lane the men would come down today. When 'the blonds' arrived the children would be thrilled. The children would tag along with them until they reached the other side of the neighbourhood, jumping up around them, laughing and touching the young men's clothes with their fingertips, in a mixture of fear and exhilaration. The children would be even happier when the men would graciously bend down, without stopping walking, to let the children touch their blond hair. The girls of the neighbourhood fell for the blonds and before long it was as though a sacred and secret covenant had been concluded between them and the local people.

'The days passed without either side daring to break the barrier of silence or ambiguity. Before the blonds appeared it would have been suicide for a stranger to enter the neighbourhood. But now the girls would stick their heads out from the balconies and windows to feast their eyes on the beauty of the two young men and sigh with the ardent passion of youth. As soon as the men were gone they would drift off in daydreams as they listened to love songs on the radio. When the blonds were coming, the girls would take their radios out on the balcony in the hope that the radio station would play a love song at just that moment, and if a love song was on they would turn the volume right up as though the song were a personal message of love from the girl with the radio. The two young men would react to all this respectfully, modestly and amiably.

'The days passed.' My grandfather gave a deep sigh and prolonged the 'a' of 'passed'.

'An old woman died,' my grandfather said. 'And fifty children were born in the neighbourhood, of skinny mothers and unemployed fathers. The summer passed and the men who sell vegetables made more money. The local women attributed to the baraka or spiritual power of the blonds the fact that their husbands, who worked sweeping the streets or as school janitors in the city centre, had all received pay rises. The husbands who had been sceptical about the baraka of the two men soon stopped scoffing when the government decided to install electricity at the beginning of winter. After all these signs of baraka the women began a campaign to plant flowers outside their front doors so that the blonds could smell the fragrance as they made their angelic passage through the Darkness district. As for the men, they filled in the puddles so the blonds would not have to walk around them.

'There was a spark of hope in the faces of the people, and this brought out their natural colour, which in the past had been coated with the grime of sadness and misery. Everyone started to make sure the children were clean, sewed new clothes for them and told them to be more polite when they met the blonds. They taught them a lovely song about birds and spring to sing when they were with the blonds.

'To reinforce all this veneration and faith, a man in the neighbourhood was suddenly appointed to an important position in the government, and he promised to pave the streets and extend the pipes to bring in drinking water. The young people told the man to ask the government to bring telephone lines to the Darkness district, and I also remember what the people did when they found out that a group of evildoers were planning to attack the blonds close to the river. They had a discussion in the mayor's house and then warned the evildoers that they and their families would be thrown out of the neighbourhood if they went ahead with their plans, and the bad guys backed down.

'No more than two years after the blonds first appeared, every wish had come true, just as miracles happen in myths and legends. The old maids got married, the muddy lanes were paved, everyone with a chronic disease was cured, most of the children passed their exams, whereas previously their results had been embarrassing. The biggest miracle of all was the overthrow of the monarchy through a coup by heroic officers who enjoyed the support of the people. It's clear that all this good fortune and felicity had come to the people by virtue of the blonds. From then on harmony and love reigned among the people of the neighbourhood, and enmity and violence almost disappeared. Another new thing was that the schools became mixed – with boys and girls together – and the government built a clinic close to the neighbourhood and I used to sell chickpeas in front of it. The government did something very logical when it changed the name from the Darkness district to the Flower district. It chose the new name after a government official visited the neighbourhood and submitted a report in which he mentioned how many flowers there were and also how clean the neighbourhood was. Almost every house had a telephone line and it was noticeable that more than a few of the inhabitants had come to have cars. The other new thing in the neighbourhood was that the old people now took part in the adult literacy programme and were enthusiastic about discovering the mysteries of the alphabet and of language in general. In short the neighbourhood acquired a new vitality and prosperity after the medicine began to take effect. But the happiness evaporated on that ill-fated morning, the day after the military coup, when the children went out to the edge of the

neighbourhood to wait for the blonds to come. They waited
long and the blonds did not come. Their mothers joined
them and sat with them on the wasteland. The government
had built a wide road across the middle of the wasteland and
now tanks and armoured personnel carriers were driving
along it. Then the rest of the local people came along to join
them, and everyone was looking at the tanks on the main
road, belching out black smoke. They had a sense of bitterness
inside them, lumps in their throats and tears in their eyes.

'The sun had set and darkness had descended again.'

My grandfather blew out the lantern flame and gave a
long sigh.

It was after midnight and the new government's tanks were
invading the neighbourhood to remove the statues of the
blonds. The men of the neighbourhood had taken up battle
positions on the roofs of the houses and in the alleyways. A
fierce battle broke out and even the women took part. I had
slipped through, along with three friends carrying grenade
launchers to destroy a tank that was moving down the middle
of the main road, but the helicopters firing from above
restricted our movements. We hid behind a taxi parked on the
pavement. Then some of the shops and other buildings
caught fire. It looked like we were doomed to lose the battle
because of the constant bombardment from the helicopters.
We broke one of the windows of the taxi and hid inside, with
plans to drive it off and escape. Suddenly one of the
helicopters in the sky burst into flames and crashed onto the
roofs of the houses. Then our fighters hit a tank with their
missiles and we saw the government troops withdrawing in
panic. A while later we saw a group of young men from the
neighbourhood rushing forward like madmen, shouting
'Allahu akbar' and spraying bullets around at random, jubilant
and heedless of the battle. We got out of the taxi when the
young men went by and we heard from them that God had
brought about a miracle. They told us the blonds had come

back to the neighbourhood and were now fighting ferociously against the government forces. They said it was the blonds alone who had set fire to the tank and brought down the helicopter. My friends cheered and shouted 'Allahu akbar' with the group as they ran towards the government troops, firing bullets in every direction. This neighbourhood was surely just a vast mental hospital. I felt anger and hatred as I stood by the taxi transfixed, watching the throngs celebrating the miraculous victory. I lit a cigarette and thought that the best way to end my torment would be to abandon this cave they call the Darkness district. Just as I turned to walk home, a torrent of missiles suddenly rained down right across the neighbourhood. One of these missiles threw me and the wreckage of the taxi against a nearby wall. I saw flames around me on all sides. I did not feel any pain but the sudden silence around me gave me a strange feeling of peace. When the blonds pulled me from under the wreckage of the car I saw that one of them was wearing a shirt stained with my blood. My father says I was unconscious when they found me in front of the door to our house but I'm sure the blonds carried me on a white stretcher and all along the way they smiled at me, and I reached out my hand to touch their beautiful blond hair.

Some of the young men from the new generation in the neighbourhood now call me the madman of Freedom Square. The government planted some trees and put some benches where the statues of the blonds had stood. They put up a large plaque with the new name of the neighbourhood: Freedom District. I know what these idiots say. They claim that the piece of shrapnel that went into my head damaged my brain. But they are just villagers still living in the Dark Ages. I have repeatedly asked the notables and others to contribute money to rebuild the statues of the blonds and protect the history of the neighbourhood. This is the least I could do to repay them the favour of saving my life. What makes me angry is that even my father no longer believes in the story of the blonds, after the soldiers demolished the statues and killed many young men that night. Some people now claim that the story of how the blonds miraculously appeared that night and fought on our side is just cheap propaganda, spread by certain youngsters to raise the moral of our fighters, and that the government army wiped out the resistance before morning broke. But I am quite sure it was the blonds who carried me on the white stretcher, and with these very fingers of mine I touched their angelic hair.

A few days ago I met a stranger whom I believe to be honest, not a fake like most of the people in the neighbourhood, and he told me he believed my story of how the blonds appeared that night. He spoke to me at length about how we have lost our history and heritage because of the agents of the West and because we have neglected our religion, and that freedom is not to become stooges in the hands of the infidels, but what I don't fully understand is the wide belt the man wrapped around my waist in his house this morning. I feel very hot because the belt is so heavy. I'll sit down in the shade of the tree... Damn, the women and children have taken all the benches.

The Corpse Exhibition

BEFORE TAKING OUT his knife he said: 'After studying the client's file you must submit a brief note on how you propose to kill your first client and how you will display his body in the city. But that doesn't mean that what you propose in your note will be approved. One of our specialists will review the proposed method and either approve it or propose a different method. This system applies to professionals in all phases of their work – even after the training phase has ended and you have taken the test. In all phases you will receive your salary in full. I don't want to go into all the details now. I'll brief you on things gradually. After you receive the client's file you cannot ask questions as you could before. You have to submit your questions in writing. All your questions, proposals and written submissions will be documented in your personal file. You absolutely may not write to me about work matters by email or call me on the phone. You will write your questions on a special form which I will provide you with later. The important thing is that you now devote your time to studying the client's file carefully and patiently. I want to reassure you that we won't stop dealing with you even if you fail in your first assignment. If you fail you'll be transferred to work in another department at the same salary. But I must remind you once again: giving up the job after you receive your first salary payment would be unacceptable and would not succeed. There are strict conditions for that, and if the management agrees to sever relations with you, you would have to undergo many tests, which could last a long time. In the archives we have files we preserve about volunteers and other agents who decided to terminate their contracts on their own initiative. If you're thinking of doing that, we'll show you some examples of the experiences of others. I'm confident you'll be able to persevere with the work and enjoy it. You'll see how your whole life will change. This is your first present, don't open it now. It's your pay in full. As for the documentaries about the lives of predatory animals, you can buy them and we'll cover the expenses later. Pay particular attention to the images of the victims' bones. Always remember, dear friend, that we are not terrorists whose aim is to bring down as many victims as possible in order to intimidate others, nor even crazy killers working for the sake of money. We have nothing to do with the fanatical Islamist groups or the intelligence agency of some nefarious government or any of that kind of nonsense. I know you now have some questions that are nagging you, but you will gradually discover that the world is built to have more than one level, and it's unrealistic for everyone to reach all the levels and all the basements with ease. Don't forget the senior positions that await you in the hierarchy of the institution if you have an imagination that is fresh, fierce and striking. Every body you finish off is a work of art waiting for you to add the final touch, so that you can shine like a precious jewel amidst the wreckage of this country. To display a corpse for others to see is the ultimate in the creativity we are seeking and which we are trying to study and benefit from. Personally I can't stand the agents who are unimaginative. We have, for example, an agent whose codename is Satan's Knife, that I wish those in charge would get rid of as soon as possible. This guy thinks that cutting off the client's limbs and hanging them from the electricity wires in the slum neighbourhoods is the height of creativity and inventiveness. He's just a conceited fool. I hate his classical methods, although he talks about a new classicism. All this lightweight does is paint the client's body parts and hang them from invisible threads, the heart in dark blue, the intestines green, the liver and testicles yellow. He does this without understanding the poetry of simplicity. When I tell you some of the details I see that puzzled look in your eyes. Calm down, breathe deep, listen to the rhythm of your secret spirit calmly and patiently. Let me explain some points to you more clearly to dispel some of the misapprehensions you may have. Let me waste some time with you. What I tell you may be just personal impressions and another member of the group may have a quite different opinion. I like concision, simplicity and the striking image. Take agent Deaf, for example. He's calm and he has a smart, lucid eye and my favourite work of his was that woman who was breastfeeding. One rainy winter's morning a crowd of passers-by and drivers stopped to look at that woman. She was naked and fat and her child, also naked, was suckling at her left breast. He put the woman under a dead palm tree in the central reservation of a busy street. There was no trace of a wound or a bullet on the woman's body or on the baby's. She and her baby looked as alive as a brook of pure water. That's a genius we lack in this century. You should have seen the woman's enormous tits and how thin the baby was, like a pile of bones painted the colour of bright white baby skin. No one could work out how the mother and her child were killed. Most people speculated that he used some mysterious poison that has not yet been classified. But you should read in the archives in our library the brief poetic report which Deaf wrote on this extraordinary work of art. He now holds an important position in the group. He deserves much more than that. You must understand properly that this country presents one of the century's rare opportunities. Our work may not last long. As soon as the situation stabilises we'll have to move onto another country. Don't worry, there are many candidates. Listen, in the past we offered new students like you classical lessons, but now things are much changed. We've started to rely on the democracy and spontaneity of the imagination, and not on instruction. I studied a long time and read many boring books justifying what we do before I was able to work professionally. We used to read studies which spoke about peace, studies written with really disgusting eloquence. There were many naïve and unnecessary analogies to justify everything. One of them was about how all the medicines at the pharmacy, even plain old toothpaste, were produced after laboratory tests on rats and other animals, so it would not be possible to bring about peace on this earth without sacrificing laboratory humans as well. Old lessons like these were boring and frustrating. Your generation is very lucky in this age of golden opportunities. A film actress licking an ice cream might give rise to dozens of photographs and news reports which reach the most remote village ravished by famine in this world, this grindstone of screaming and dancing. This at least achieves what I call 'the justice of discovering the insignificance and equivocal essence of the world.' How much more so a corpse displayed creatively in the city centre! Perhaps I've told you too much but let me tell you frankly that I'm worried about you, because you're either an idiot or a genius, and agents like that excite my curiosity. If you're a genius that would be gratifying. I still believe in genius although most members of the group talk about experience and practice. And if you're an idiot, let me tell you before I go a short and useful story about one idiot who naïvely tried to mess with us. I didn't even like his nickname -- 'the Nail'. After the committee had approved the way the Nail proposed to kill his client and display his body in a large restaurant, we waited for results. But this guy was very slow about finishing off his work. I met him several times and asked him what was causing the delay. He would say that he didn't want to repeat the methods of his predecessors and was thinking of bringing about a creative quantum leap in our work. But the truth was different. The Nail was a coward who had been infected with banal humanitarian feelings and, like any sick man, had started to question the benefit of killing others and wondering whether there was some creator monitoring all our deeds, and that was the beginning of the abyss. Because every child born in this world is simply a possibility, either to be good or evil, according to the classification set by schools of religious education in this stupid world. But it's a completely different matter for us. Every child that's born is just an extra burden on the ship that's about to sink. Anyway, let me tell you what happened to the Nail. He had a relative who worked as a guard in the hospital in the city centre, and the Nail was thinking of slipping into the hospital mortuary and choosing a corpse instead of making a corpse himself. It was easy to carry that off after he'd given his relative half the pay he'd received from the group. The mortuary was full of corpses from those stupid acts of terrorism, bodies ripped apart by car bombs, others which had their heads cut off in sectarian feuds, bloated bodies from the river bed, and many other stupid ones that had been finished off in random murders which had nothing to do with art. The Nail slipped into the mortuary that night and started looking for the right cadaver to display to the public. The Nail was looking for the children's corpses because in his first report he had proposed an idea which involved killing a five-year-old child.

'In the mortuary there were specimens of school children who had been mutilated by car bombs, or incinerated in some street market or broken into pieces after planes bombed houses. Finally the Nail chose a child who had been beheaded along with the rest of his family for sectarian reasons. The body was clean and the cut at the neck was as neat as a piece of torn paper. The Nail thought of exhibiting this body in a restaurant and putting the eyes of the other family members on the table served in bowls of blood, like a soup. Maybe it was a beautiful idea but before all else his work would have been a cheat and a betrayal. If he had beheaded the child himself it would have been an authentic work of art but to steal it from the mortuary and act in this despicable manner would be a disgrace and cowardice at the same time. But he did not understand that the world today is linked together by more than a tunnel and a corridor. It was the mortician who caught the Nail before he was able to deceive the poor public. The mortician was in his early sixties, an enormous man. His work in the mortuary had flourished after the increase in the number of mutilated bodies in the country. People sought him out to patch together the bodies of their children and other relatives who were torn apart in explosions and random killings. They would pay handsomely to have him restore their children to the appearance by which they originally knew them. The mortician was truly a great artist. He worked with patience and with great love. That night he guided the Nail into a side room in the mortuary and locked the door on him. He injected him with some drug, which paralysed him without making him unconscious. He laid him out on the mortuary table, strapped his hands and legs down and gagged his mouth. He was humming a pretty children's song in his strange woman's voice as he prepared his work table. It was a song about a child fishing for a frog in a small puddle of blood, and every now and then he would stroke the Nail's hair tenderly and whisper in his ear: "Ooh, my dear, ooh, my friend, there is something stranger than death – to look at the world, which is looking at you, but without any gesture or understanding or even purpose, as though you and the world are united in blindness, like silence and loneliness. And there is something a little stranger than death: a man and a woman playing in bed, and then you come, just you, you who always miswrite the story of your life."

'The mortician finished his work in the early morning.

'In front of the gate of the Ministry of Justice there was a platform like the platforms on which the city's statues stand, but made of a pulp of flesh and bones. On top of the platform stood a pillar of bronze and from the pillar hung the Nail's skin, complete and detached from his flesh with great skill, waving like a flag of victory. In the front part of the platform you could clearly see the Nail's right eye, set in the pulp of his flesh. It had a look rather like the insipid look your eyes have now. Do you know who the mortician was? He's the man in charge of the most important department in the institution. He's the man in charge of the truth and creativity department.'

Then he thrust the knife into my stomach and said: 'You're shaking.'

The Market of Stories

IN RESPONSE TO invitations from the critics among his few friends, he would quote the Hungarian novelist Béla Hamvas: 'While at home, you get to know the world, but on the road, yourself.' Khaled al-Hamrani had never left his home town and now he had reached the age of fifty-seven. In fact he had not written a single story that did not take place around the street market close to his house. So far three collections of his stories had come out, published at his private expense, all of them set in the market.

In a curious interview with him in one of the local newspapers, he said: 'You can turn the woman who sells fish in the market into a spaceship lost in the cosmos, or turn aubergines into a philosophy lesson. The important thing is to observe at length, like someone contemplating committing suicide from a balcony. The other important thing is to have an imagination which is not melodramatic but malicious and extremely serious, and to have an ascetic spirit that is close to death. This street market that I write about is a vast ocean as far as I am concerned, and I am just a bubble which doubtless exists but which cannot be seen clearly.' Asked if his stories were much alike and boring because the market alone was their 'magic box', he spoke straight: 'What I detest is looking for new experiences and places in order to say the same thing, because the whole world is reflected in the eyes of a single child, is it not? Or even in the blood of a chicken slaughtered in the market. (Hamrani laughs and then continues derisively). I am not looking for myself. I want to swim in one lake and I'm certain it's the whole universe...'

Khaled al-Hamrani woke early that day as if emerging from a well. He immediately grabbed a pen, and without rising from his bed enthusiastically scribbled numbers on the wall. His wife was still snoring beside him and the children were also still sleeping. Since the sharp increase in random bombings and killings in Baghdad, no one in the house got up early any more. The children left school, and only play outside the house for a short period per day. Al-Hamrani's wife no longer goes to visit her family, and does not even go shopping. They have a small amount of money which al-Hamarani saved from his job as a grape juice vendor on al-Rashid Street.

Hamrani sat on the edge of the bed contemplating the five numbers gravely and with suspicion. It was the first time he had had a dream connected with numbers. He thought the numbers would disappear as soon as he got out of bed, but as he made tea he felt they were going to radiate into his brain like five hot cinders. He noticed a light but annoying morning breeze trying to blow open the small kitchen window. He was sitting on the carpet on the ground with his legs stretched out, drinking the tea. He tried to pull together again all the images in the dream but there was only one image – him standing in front of a vast wall eroded by damp, with the numbers written in fluorescent blue. He had felt a horrible pain in his knees as he stood transfixed in front of the wall. What could these numbers be? Hamrani pondered this question, though he didn't give much thought to the wall itself. We attribute some of our dreams to our experiences in life, and Hamrani had written before, in his secret unpublished autobiography, about his memory of a wall from the days of his childhood. He felt embarrassed about writing his autobiography but he was an obsessive reader of what others wrote about their own lives:

In my childhood, in 1983, the wing of an Iranian warplane fell on the lane next to ours. The air defences had hit the plane, one of five that had attacked the oil fields. Another part of the plane fell on a watermelon farm. We were living in a government district in the oil city of Kirkuk, in houses the government had built for people associated with the army, all of the same design – a bedroom, a reception room, a bathroom and toilet and a small back garden. The adults were talking about a girl whose brain was stuck to the wall after the wing fell and blocked the lane. The wing destroyed the front of several houses. All the children in the neighbourhood heard about the girl's brain. In school one boy said the girl's headless body flew high into the sky and never came down. After the wing incident I changed the route I took to come back home, making a diversion to this lane. I would pull myself together, then set off down the lane as fast as possible to see the girl's brain. But I didn't see it every time. I would rush along, unable to bring myself to turn to the wall where the brain was stuck, and wondering whether – as I had heard – they had washed it away. Fear made me approach the source of my fear and run away from it at the same time.

Was there some connection between the numbers and the wing of the plane and the girl's brain? The numbers were 3, 14, 9, 2 and 22. Perhaps they were someone's telephone number. No, they definitely weren't that, because they didn't fit the pattern of landline numbers or mobile numbers. The sum of the numbers was 50, so it wasn't a prediction of the year when he would die.

He told his wife of the numbers dream when they were having breakfast with the children. She smiled and said: 'Let's hope it's a good sign. Numbers in dreams mean that money is on the way, so let's hope it's a good sign. Right, Abu Fatima, so on your way from the market today bring half a kilo of meat and a kilo of onions. Right, and don't forget Hassan's shoes. You know, the feast's in four days.'

As he wandered around the market, observing the chaos

of it, which rarely resolved into any kind of order, Hamrani thought he ought to reread the story of the oranges which he had written a week ago and not confuse his mind by looking for a new story. Or perhaps thinking about the numbers was preventing him from concentrating on foraging for new material for stories. I should explain to you that his stories were not very interesting to most readers, not even to those who called themselves, especially after the fall of the dictator, the educated elite of writers and artists. Because literature in this country is a literature that goes through phases. Since the fall of Saddam Hussein there have been incessant calls for writing to be intelligible, realistic, factual and pragmatic. They are lamenting over readers who don't exist. They claim that the writers of the past made the readers defect, whereas in fact for hundreds of years there were no readers in the country, in the broad sense of the word. There were only hungry people, killers, illiterates, soldiers, villagers, people who prayed, people who were lost and people who were oppressed. Our writers seem to have grown tired of writing for each other. They also hold the Saddam Hussein period responsible for the prevalence of obscure literature and for exaggerated experimentalism, as though obscurity and experimentation were offences or a Baathist invention. They are civil servants looking for a new role for themselves in this phase. They are 'phase writers' who now want to pounce on all the roles. They claim that they are construction workers who will rebuild what war destroyed, that they are cultured politicians and economists, surgeons, pundits of disaster and iconoclasts destroying religious idols and superstitions. But Hamrani was the kind of writer who did not understand what phases mean. What mattered to him, he said, was the essence of Man – a truth that phases cannot distort or change. So Hamrani's stories, according to the classification of the advocates of the new phase, would be experimental and obscure. Let's take for example his story 'The Name of the Orange'. Hamrani picked up this story in the market when he caught sight of a young woman wearing a black abaya, and the bag of oranges she was holding ripped and the oranges rolled into the mud. It's true that at first he assumes that the young woman is a terrorist who is going to blow herself up in the market, which draws in the reader and arouses his curiosity, especially as many men deep inside see a woman as a cunt, a bum and tits, an appetising piece of flesh designed for fucking and cooking, and such a suicide might be an offence to their manhood, although even the idea of a woman's flesh being torn apart might serve as a joke to titillate the man's cock. One day Hamrani heard an appalling joke from the man who sells sweets. The man said a friend of his sold fish in another street market and he found the suicide bomber's cunt among the fish after she blew herself up with a bomb belt that day. In fact it was the man's wife who found the vulva when the man took his goods back home. His wife asked him for a logical explanation for why there was a young woman's cunt among the fish. That's a type of popular gibberish that stems from a long history of violence, oppression and destruction, not an example of expressive irony by citizens who belong to a modern city. It's primitive tribal gibberish which tries to hide behind tasteless and gory laughter.

But Hamrani quickly transported his reader to another world through the images which suddenly appear in his stories, to change the course of the narrative or of the language itself. This is what would throw the reader and turn the critics of the new phase against him. In the story of the oranges, for example, he says that before she reached the market the suicide woman, wearing her black abaya, was walking along an abandoned dirt track, completely naked, carrying an orange tree on her back like a cross. He says that whip lashes had left stripes on the naked woman's skin. The strange thing is that after that Hamrani, like an impressionist painter, goes into great detail about the woman's fingers as she picks the oranges out of the mud. Hamrani's critics may be right and he too just spouts gibberish all year round.

Hamrani sat down next to the man who sells tea, whose customers sit in front of him on a low wooden platform in the shape of an arc. He smoked three cigarettes with the cup of tea, and the numbers were turning in his mind and troubling him. The tea-man was telling his customers about the police patrol which found twenty severed heads in front of the door to the Salam mosque. The man turned on a small tape recorder and it played a popular song celebrating the breasts of a young woman. A fat man in a dishdasha was telling the tea-man about the latest lottery draw, which was won by a poor man who lived in a house made of metal sheeting. The fat man said: 'Your lot in life is in heaven and you don't know what it is.' Hamrani smiled at an idea which occurred to him. Perhaps whoever lives in heaven had sent him the lucky numbers as a free gift. The numbers would work in the lottery. Hamrani knew a shop in the middle of the market which sold lottery tickets. Why shouldn't he try out the numbers in the lottery? It would be amusing, and exciting too. But what if a miracle happened and his ticket won? Certainly people would try hard to dream the lucky numbers at night and psychiatrists might intervene to help the dreamers. It was not unusual for Hamrani to get into foolish conversations with himself. He knew that we all, like human rags, imagine and say to ourselves day and night things that are degenerate, even alarming. The important thing is that the hallucination should continue, that the viper of time should bite the ephemeral people who visit the field, that in all our life we should write one story or poem: 'This market is my world, my grave and my wings. I am the house of worms that is troubled by a number in a dream.'

In front of the shop which sold lottery tickets the fantasy that Hamrani had created in his mind for amusement was dashed. All the lottery tickets needed six or seven numbers but his dream had provided him with only the five numbers, for which he was trying to find a place in the chaos of this world. Five numbers which added to the mystery instead of opening a door. He cut a path through the market crowd as the traders greeted him loudly and joked with him. They all had a good relationship with this steady customer, who shopped for stories to preserve on paper. Then the five numbers vanished from his mind. He watched an old man selling pictures of religious personalities. The only thing the subjects of the pictures had in common was the turbans on their heads. He also saw a young man wearing a strange red shirt, carrying a collection of jeans, with a cigarette in his mouth. The man offered him a pair of black jeans and said he would sell them at half-price because he wanted to sell all the jeans for no profit and then find another job. This is a well-known way of attracting customers and the young man had been doing it for more than two years. It was the same with the story of how cheap his jeans were, and when one of them reminded him that he had heard the same story about jeans before, the man smiled and said: 'Are you going to buy or aren't you?'

Hamrani bought a new pair of shoes for his young son Hassan, then he bought one and a half kilos of onions. He was looking for the people who sold kids' bags, thinking he might use one to wrap the shoes. The sky shed a few drops as a warning of rain to come. He raised his face to the sky when a gentle drop of water wet the end of his nose. The last thing he saw was the leaden sky thick with cloud and three birds hovering high. Then the truck bomb parked near the market exploded, like a giant volcano.

They say his body was ripped in three. The legs and trunk were in one place, one arm was in a pile of blackened tomatoes, and his head, part of his shoulder and his right arm were close to the man selling jeans who, because of the storm of fire and iron, turned into a small monkey drawn in charcoal with no features. The strange thing is that all Hamrani's brothers and other relatives reported that only with great effort could they prise apart the fingers of Hamrani's right hand to free the shoe he had bought for Hassan his son. The other shoe was lost in the pile of debris. For sure these details are insultingly meaningless. Maybe they are like my attempt to make a link between the five numbers and the day the truck-bomb blew up. What cryptic message lay in these numbers? More than seventy people were killed in the market that day, another number that has nothing to do with Hamrani's dream. When a whole people or a group of people face an accumulation of many years of war, terror, poverty and destruction, then looking for illogical or even trivial details is tantamount to mumbo jumbo, but there always remains the human need to explain events by a logic other than that of cold reason, which attributes effects to their supposed causes, a noble human need. Perhaps mumbo jumbo and writing stories are also a sad human embrace of the inscrutability of the world.

Today I finished painting the bedroom walls light blue and all that remained was the spot where the five numbers were written in pencil. The situation in Baghdad has now improved and I still see the vast world of the market as material for my stories. Two years have passed since the numbers dream and the nightmare about me dying in the market. Good. With another brush stroke the five numbers will vanish beneath the paint but what cannot vanish is my great fear of dreams and nightmares. I cannot believe that when we die at night we come back every morning as we were, without a mysterious dust coating us. Last night I dreamt of a sheep's head talking about the sun.

Ali's Bag

WHEN THE STATUE of Saddam Hussein came down in Baghdad, a vicious brawl broke out in the TV room. Six young Sudanese had a fight with a group of Iraqis who were celebrating the fall of the dictator. It was a remark by Youssef the Sudanese that lit the spark: 'The American troops will fuck your women, so why are you so cheerful?'

The Afghans and some young Nigerians tried to break up the brawl. As for the Iranians, they left the room and started to watch through the windows. Blood was shed and one young Sudanese was taken to hospital after he fractured his skull and lost consciousness. By the time the riot police arrived there was a horrible smell coming from the room and the furniture was completely smashed. I watched the battle coolly from the door. I had spent more than three years in this refugee reception centre in this small Italian town and I had seen many furious fights. They could break out over washing powder or a pair of women's underwear. That's what happened with Parvin the Kurdish woman's pants. Parvin told the Kurdish refugees she had seen a young Pakistani man steal her underwear from the clothes line. Thereupon a battle of honour broke out between the Pakistanis and the Kurds and it did not stop for three days. The manager of the centre called in the police when the guards at the centre failed to stop the fighting.

What aroused my curiosity in the battle of the TV room was Ali al-Basrawi. He was hugging his bag and grinning like a madman. This delicate young man had changed completely since he came to the centre. I invited him that evening to

have a coffee in my room to make sure he was well and say
goodbye to him. He had decided to continue his travels to
Finland and I was not fully convinced he had made the right
decision. I advised him to go to Germany or any other
country where maybe he would have a better chance of
finding work. We spoke at length that evening about his
dreams, his fears and his plans. He told me he could hear his
mother's voice. She was speaking to him lovingly and giving
him advice, but she was also reproaching him for what
happened to her head in the Greek forest. He too was happy
that the dictator had fallen, though he was worried by the
thought that the European countries might stop granting
asylum to Iraqis. I told him that things might change in Iraq
and we might be able to go back to our homes and our
families, but he reminded me of his black bag and said: 'I have
no family, no friends and no hope. Everything I possess I've
been carrying in my bag. I'm hoping I can take my mother
to a place that's safe and comfortable, because the poor
woman has suffered long enough.'

More than once it has occurred to me that I will spend
my life writing about the events and surreal happenings I
have experienced along the routes taken by undocumented
migrants. It's my cancer and I do not know how it can be
cured. I'm afraid I might meet a comic end like the Iraqi
writer Khalid al-Hamrani, who spent his whole life writing
about the street market close to his house. When the market
was demolished and blocks of flats were built in its place,
Hamrani killed himself, leaving six collections of stories, all of
them about the world of the market. Once I was talking to a
young German novelist about my personal experiences in the
world of migrants and my ideas about turning what I had
lived through into material for literary fiction. When it was
the young German's turn to speak he told me that he had
never written anything of merit and that his youth and lack
of experiences in life were the reason for this failure. I felt he
wanted to tell me that he envied me the strange and painful

life experiences I had had. But what he said, instead of making me feel privileged, severely embarrassed me. His remarks reminded me once again what a broken and insignificant creature I really was. I was overwhelmed by a bitter sense of shame, like the man that the Russian film-maker Andrei Tarkovsky talks about: a man who has an accident in the street and has his arm cut off, and when the passers-by gather round him waiting for the ambulance to arrive, the man takes out a handkerchief and and puts it on his arm in an attempt to hide it from the gaze of the onlookers.

But I was always tempted to write the story of Ali al-Basrawi, even if it is loaded with grief and gloom, along with a few Third World clichés which try to appeal to the sentiments of Western audiences. Whenever I thought of the story, it reaffirmed the poetic nature of the human face hidden like a jewel under the millions of tonnes of this trivial life's rubbish. Perhaps because I am a poet and live as a refugee in a place like this, a cattle pen, I have a hard heart or perhaps a brain with a trace of a fatuous belief in absurdity, a brain which tries through meagre words to express its anger and interest in human terror at the same time. But whenever I looked at a tree or contemplated a night filled with the wolves of doubt, my heart was overwhelmed by a flood of naïve and childish sadness. I believe that writing should not be handicapped by the banal emotions that emanate from human masses like the smell of sweat from their shirts and that are all identical, like a row of toilets in one bathroom. But Ali's story seeped into my blood and could bring tears to my eyes on many nights. I wept that my heart had turned to stone and I wept because the world is much purer and more beautiful than it appears.

When Ali al-Basrawi arrived at the refugee centre last year there was a great commotion. The refugees had a riotous time laughing and making jokes about what his black bag might contain. It was a travel bag of a design that dated back to the 1950s. As soon as Ali arrived the officials called the police, who detained him for three days and then released him, but they returned his bag to him only after three months. In the meantime the bag was examined in laboratories in the capital and the manager of the centre was stunned to hear that it was returned with all its contents.

In the 1990s Ali was living with his seven brothers, all of them older than him, in one of the miserable districts of Basra. His father worked as a night watchman at several shops in the city centre and his mother, like most Iraqi mothers, was a creature on whom was dumped all the muck of injustice, sadness and human brutality. She was the victim of a depraved male world beyond hope. It would be easy to forget that God exists if you could experience a single day in the life of an Iraqi mother. This might seem like just a naïve and romantic sentiment, but if there were hidden cameras exposing to the world the abhorrent things that happen to a woman in Iraqi homes, then the very stones would speak out to denounce the state of affairs and curse whoever brought it about. Ali's brothers had inherited from their father an addiction to imposing on their mother all the problems and misfortunes of poverty and fate. She would be beaten for the most trivial reason and the mother would repeatedly rebuke her Lord for failing to provide her with a daughter to help with the housework and sympathise with her. Ali could not easily forget the day when his eldest brother punched and kicked the poor woman until she was unconscious because she forgot to wake him up to go to market to look for work. The mother's only response to all the brutality and insults was to sit near the old wardrobe and cry, imploring the righteous saints to save her from the iniquity. Ali was a boy at the time, and his mother hugged him and sobbed. She might have been hugging a child who would grow up to beat her.

Ali says that when she tired of crying she would take from the wardrobe her small bag, the only thing she possessed – an old travel bag which contained a wooden comb, a mirror, a picture of the Imam Ali, a Quran wrapped in a piece of green cloth and a black-and-white photograph of her when she was young, sitting with her father on the waterfront. She would undo her black headscarf and start to comb her white hair idiotically for a full hour as she hummed the tune of an old song about sympathy for one's mother. But perhaps the woman's constant prayers to be released from this life did find listeners among the devils in heaven, because she suddenly died of a stroke, and after her death Ali would have to wait years before he could get revenge on his brothers and his father, that pile of shit that now lives paralysed in his wheelchair.

Ali planned everything quietly and carefully for more than a year. He decided to flee to Iran first and on the night of his departure he went into his mother's room, took her bag and slipped away. His friend Adnan was waiting for him at the end of the lane carrying a pickaxe and a shovel in a sack. The two friends lit cigarettes and set off towards the cemetery. The sky was clear and a moon as big as Ali's fear shed its light on the grave as the two friends dug it up. With a piece of orange cloth Ali cleaned his mother's bones, then put them in the old bag.

Ali picked up the bag with his mother inside and fled to Iran, happy to have his revenge. He imagined how everyone's face would be as pale as death when they discovered what had happened. He never parted with the bag of bones throughout his next journey to Turkey across the mountains. He would sleep in the valleys with the other migrants, hugging the bag close with love and veneration. His strange bag, and the obsessive way he guarded it, gave rise to amusement and derision, but he took no notice of that and he did not reveal to anyone the secret of the bag. For a year he worked in Istanbul in a balloon factory so that he could continue his journey as a migrant, and for that year Ali would talk to his mother at night about the distant country that he would choose to live in peacefully, and about how he wanted

63

to start a new life and forget about all the torment. But Ali could not easily get over the enormity of what he had done. He would often get goosebumps and sharp stomach pains when he thought about it. Fear of the unknown, mixed with fear of remorse, wrenched at his heart.

Before the cruellest days of cold descended on Istanbul Ali made a deal with a smuggler to travel with him on foot across the Greek–Turkish border. Winter is the best season for crossing borders because the border guards grow too lazy to go out on their daily patrols. Ali was worried about the river they would have to cross, but the smuggler reassured him, telling him they would make the crossing in a boat big enough for everyone, as it would be impossible to swim in the cold water. Ali bought some plastic bags nonetheless and wrapped his mother's bones in them. His fears were misplaced and the smuggler did not make them swim across the river, the way you hear in stories about dishonest smugglers. Instead it was the forest that would bring Ali to grief, through an event which gave him pangs of conscience and dragged him into a deep depression.

As soon as the group set off into the forest behind the smuggler, some border guards appeared and began shouting at the group, ordering them to stop. But the smuggler urged the group to run behind him as fast as possible. They fled between the trees in the darkness of the thick forest, letting the branches scratch their faces and rip their winter coats. Ali was running as fast as he could, clutching the bag to his chest and trying to keep up with the smuggler so he would not lose his way. But he crashed into a tree trunk, was knocked backwards and fell to the ground, and his mother's bones flew in all directions in the darkness of the forest. Ali bent down to the ground, bleeding from the forehead and trying in fear and confusion to gather the scattered bones. He felt the bones carefully before putting them back in the bag. He wiped the blood from his eyes and staggered on again, as the guards shouted in the distance from time to time.

Miraculously the group escaped the ambush set by the border guards, thanks to the smuggler's intelligence and knowledge of the paths through the forest, though a young Iranian and a Kurd lost their way and may have been caught. The rest of the group reached the capital Athens safely and the smuggler handed them over to an old Greek man who would take them across the sea to Italy.

While Ali was staying in a house in Athens for trafficking migrants, he checked his bag. His mother's bones, the mirror, the wooden comb, the picture of the Imam Ali and the Quran were all in place, but what was missing was her head, which used to rub cheeks with his as she watered it with her tears and tortured sobs...

Ali will definitely take his bag of bones to a safe place where he can bury them, a place which no one else can find, and maybe he alone will hear one of the songs sung by his mother, whose head went missing in that forest.

The Truck to Berlin

THIS STORY TOOK place in darkness and if I were destined to write it again, I would record only the cries of terror which rang out at the time and the other mysterious noises that accompanied the massacre. A major part of the story would make a good experimental radio piece. For sure most readers would see the story as merely a fabrication by the author or maybe as a modest allegory for horror. But I see no need to swear an oath in order for you to believe in the strangeness of this world. What I need to do is write this story, like a shit stain on a nightshirt, or perhaps a stain in the form of a wild flower.

In the summer of 2000 I was working in a bar in the middle of Istanbul. My broken English helped me in the job, since the customers were tourists, mostly Germans who also spoke laughable English. At the time I was on the run from the hell of the years of economic sanctions, not out of fear of hunger or of Saddam Hussein. In fact I was on the run from myself and from other monsters. In those cruel years fear of the unknown helped obliterate the sense of belonging to a familiar reality and brought to the surface a savagery which had been buried beneath a man's simple daily needs. In those years a vile and bestial cruelty prevailed, driven by fear of dying from starvation. I felt I was in danger of turning into a rat.

I saved some money from my work and paid it to those who smuggle the human cattle of the East to the farms of the West. There were ways of smuggling that differed in price: travelling by air on a forged passport, which was very costly, and walking with the smuggler through forests and rivers on the borders, which was the cheapest way. There was the sea route and the truck route, which I had considered, though I was disturbed by stories of the device the police use to measure the level of carbon dioxide in the trucks to detect the breath of those hiding inside them. But it was not that device which made me abandon the idea of travelling by truck, but rather the story of Ali the Afghan and the massacre on the truck to Berlin. The Afghan was a treasure trove of smuggling stories. He had lived in Istanbul illegally for ten years. He worked in forgery and selling drugs, to spend what he earned on Russian prostitutes and bribing the police. Some people have ridiculed me for believing the story of the truck to Berlin. In fact I have more than one reason for believing such stories. Because in my view the world is very fragile, frightening and inhumane. All it needs is a little shake for its hideous nature and its primeval fangs to emerge. Obviously you already know many similarly tragic stories of migration and its horrors from the media, which have focused first and foremost on migrants drowning. My view is that as far as the public is concerned such mass drownings are an enjoyable film scene, like a new Titanic. The media do not, for example, carry reports of black comedy, just as you do not read stories about what the armies of European democracies do when at night, in a vast forest, they catch a group of terrified humans, drenched in rain, hungry and cold. I have seen how the Bulgarian police beat a young Pakistani with a spade until he lost consciousness. Then in the bitterest cold they asked us all to get into a river that was almost frozen over. That was before they handed us over to the Turkish army.

Ali the Afghan says that there were thirty-five young Iraqis, dreaming youngsters who had made a deal with a Turkish smuggler to carry them in a closed truck exporting tinned fruit from Istanbul to Berlin. The deal was this: everyone would pay $4,000 for a trip that would last just

68

seven days; the truck would travel by night and spend the day stopped at small border towns; anyone who wanted to take a shit would have to do that during the daytime; pissing would be allowed during the night in empty water bottles; no one could carry a mobile phone during the trip; everyone must keep silent and breathe quietly while the truck was stopped at border posts or traffic controls, and there should be absolutely no quarrelling. But what worried the Berlin truck group was the story published in the Turkish newspapers a few days earlier about a group of Afghans who paid an Iranian smuggler large sums of money to carry them by truck to Greece. The truck drove for a full night. At daybreak it stopped and the smuggler told them to get out quietly because they had reached a Greek border town. The Afghans got out of the truck hugging their bags, feeling a mixture of joy and fear, and sat down under a giant tree. The smuggler said they were in a small Greek wood and all they had to do was wait till the morning and, when the Greek police turned up, they should immediately apply for asylum. In the morning the newspapers published a picture of the Afghans sitting in a public garden in the middle of Istanbul. The truck had driven them around the streets of Istanbul all night and had not even left the suburbs. As in all stories of fraud and deception, the Iranian and his truck vanished and the Afghans were thrown in jail pending deportation.

But the Berlin truck group had no choice but to take the risk. To be frightened of stories of fraud would mean paralysis, losing hope and going back to a country where hunger and injustice were rife. They also relied on the reputation of the famous smuggler, who they were told was the best and most honest smuggler in all Turkey. So far he had never failed and had not tricked anyone. He was a pious man and had performed the haj pilgrimage three times, and so was called Haj Ibrahim.

Haj Ibrahim's truck left Istanbul by night, after the 'customers' had loaded up with food and bottles of water. The dark and heat inside the truck was intense, though air did leak inside through small invisible holes. For fear that the air would run out, the young men were breathing rapidly, like someone preparing to dive into a river. After five hours of travel, the smell of bodies, sweaty socks and the spicy food they were eating in the darkness made it even stuffier. But the first night was a success. In the morning the truck stopped at a garage in a border village. The back door was opened and the customers could breathe again, their hopes renewed. The garage was a former cowshed and two young men supervised the shitting operation. The travellers were not allowed to get off the truck, let alone go into the village or anywhere else. One of the two young men took them in turn to a small and very dirty toilet in the corner of the cowshed, while the other bought food and water for them and came back at the end of the day.

On the second night there was a Mercedes car which drove well ahead of the Berlin truck to check the road and provide the truck driver with information. The Berlin truck drove in peace all the second night, making only three very short stops. In the morning they took them this time to a large garage which had other trucks and it was easy to hear the noise of the town.

On the third night a military jeep drove ahead of the truck to secure the route. In this stage of the trip the truck drove only five hours, before it suddenly stopped, turned and retraced its path at high speed. In the darkness of the truck the young men were discouraged and could feel the driver's panic in the crazy way he was driving. They started to grumble and some of them recited prayers and verses of the Quran to themselves or under their breath. One young man kept repeating the Throne Verse of the Quran out loud. He had a beautiful voice, but it was marred by his plaintive tone, which added to the dismay of the other travellers. The truck drove at this speed for close to an hour, then stopped again. A quarter of an hour later the journey resumed at a moderate speed, but the young men could not make out which direction they were moving in: some favoured the idea that they were going back, others believed they were continuing the journey. They thought it was the smuggling mafias that were giving instructions to the driver by mobile phone, depending on the road conditions and dangers such as police patrols. Then the passengers felt that the truck had started to drive along a winding dirt road. The truck suddenly came to a halt, the driver turned off the engine and an eerie and mysterious silence reigned inside the truck to Berlin, a satanic silence that would bring forth a miracle and a story hard to believe.

The thirty-five young men waited in the darkness of the truck more than three hours, whispering to each other about what had happened. Some of them tried to peek out of the very small holes near the back door. Their watches showed 7.10 in the morning, time to stock up on water. They still had enough food but the water would run out quickly, and then there was the need to take a shit. That's how the unrest began. Some of them started to kick the sides of the truck and shout out to anyone outside. Three of them objected and asked the others to keep quiet. The smell of strife hung in the meagre and electric air. They could see each other only as dark shadows and could tell each other apart only by judging the direction of someone's voice. By midday almost everyone was banging on the walls and back door of the truck and calling out for help. Some shat in food bags, and the repulsive smell built up inside the truck like strata of rock. The young men's breathing, taken together, was like that of a monster roaring in the dark. The fear and the smell so shattered everyone's nerves that quarrelling and fistfights broke out in the gloom. The fighting spread, then after an hour died down because thirst had restored the calm. Everyone sat around whispering and speculating in low voices, like a hive of bees. Every now and then one of them would curse or kick the walls of the truck. At this stage most of the young men were making sure they had hidden in their bags what food and water they had left.

Despite the pitch black, which made it impossible to tell a face from a foot, some of them did things which were not really necessary under the circumstances. One would tie up his shoelaces, another would take off his watch and hide it in his pocket, and a third would change his shirt in the dark. Such is the imagination of man, which is strangely active in situations such as this, and acts like an alarm bell or a hallucinogenic drug.

On the third day there was complete chaos. Some young men who still had the energy to hang on to life tried to break down the truck door, while others kept shouting and banging on the walls. One of them was begging and pleading for a gulp of water. The sound of farts and insults. Quranic verses and prayers recited in loud voices. Some were overcome with despair and sat thinking about their lives like patients about to die. The smells were unbearable, enough to exterminate more than one flock of the birds hovering over their heads. I am not writing now about those sounds and smells which come and go along the paths of secret migration, but about that resounding scream which suddenly burst from the chaos. It sounded like an unknown force which transformed the uproar and chaos of the truck into a cruel layer of ice. Then there reigned an intense and cloying silence which made it possible to hear the heartbeat of every traveller. It was a scream that emerged from caves whose secrets have never been unravelled. When they heard the scream, they tried to imagine the source of this voice, neither human nor animal, which had rocked the darkness of the truck.

It seemed that the cruelty of man, the cruelty of animals and legendary monsters had condensed and together had started to play a hellish tune.

After four days the Serbian police came across the truck on the edge of a small border town surrounded by forest on all sides. The truck was in an abandoned poultry field. It's not important now what happened to the smugglers, for all these stories are similar. Perhaps the smugglers found out that the police were watching their movements and wanted to hide a few days, or perhaps it was for some trivial reason connected with disputes between the smuggling mafias over money.

When the policemen opened the back door of the truck, a young man soaked in blood jumped down from inside and ran like a madman towards the forest. The police chased him but he disappeared into the vast forest. In the truck there were thirty-four bodies. They had not been torn apart with knives or any other weapon. Rather it was the claws and beaks of eagles, the teeth of crocodiles and other unknown instruments that had been at work on them. The truck was full of shit and piss and blood, livers ripped apart, eyes gouged out, intestines just as though hungry wolves had been there. Thirty-four young men had become a large soggy mass of flesh, blood and shit.

No one believed the story which Jankovic, the Serbian policeman told. In fact they made fun of him. Those who were with him there did not corroborate his account, though they did agree with him about the bloodstained youth who ran off into the forest. The Serbian newspapers asked why the youth disappeared but the police claimed that he crossed the border into Hungary.

In bed Jankovic looks at the ceiling and speaks to his wife: 'I'm not mad, woman. I tell you for the thousandth time. As soon as the man reached the forest he started to run on all fours, then turned into a grey wolf, before he vanished...'

The Nightmares of Carlos Fuentes

IN IRAQ HIS name was Salim Abdul Husain and he worked for the municipality in the cleaning department, part of a group assigned by the manager to clear up in the aftermath of explosions. He died in Holland in 2009 under another name: Carlos Fuentes.

Bored and disgusted as on every miserable day, Salim and his colleagues were sweeping a street market after a petrol tanker had exploded nearby, incinerating chickens, fruit and vegetables, and some people. They were sweeping the market slowly and cautiously for fear they might sweep up with the debris any human body parts left over. But they were always looking for an intact wallet or perhaps a gold chain, a ring or a watch which could still tell the time. Salim was not as lucky as his colleagues in finding the valuables left over from death. He needed money to buy a visa to go to Holland and escape this hell of fire and death. His only lucky find was a man's finger with a valuable silver ring of great beauty. Salim put his foot over the finger, bent down carefully, and with disgust pulled the silver ring off. He picked up the finger and put it in a black bag where they collected all the body parts. The ring ended up on Salim's finger and he would contemplate the gemstone in surprise and wonder, and in the end he abandoned the idea of selling it. Might one say that he felt a secret spiritual relationship with the ring?

When he applied for asylum in Holland he also applied to change his name: from Salim Abdul Husain to Carlos

Fuentes. He explained his request to the official in the immigration department on the grounds that he was frightened of the fanatical Islamist groups, because his request for asylum was based on his work as a translator for the U.S. forces and his fear that someone might assassinate him as a traitor to his country. Salim had consulted his cousin who lived in France about changing his name. He called him on his mobile from the immigration department because Salim had no clear idea of a new foreign name that would suit him. In his flat in France his cousin was taking a deep drag on a joint when Salim called. Suppressing a laugh, his cousin said: 'You're quite right. It's a hundred times better to be from Senegal or China than it is to have an Arab name in Europe. But you couldn't possibly have a name like Jack or Stephen, I mean a European name. Perhaps you should choose a brown name – a Cuban or Argentine name would suit your complexion, which is the colour of burnt barley bread.' His cousin was looking through a pile of newspapers in the kitchen as he continued the conversation on the phone, and he remembered that two days earlier he had read a name, perhaps a Spanish name, in a literary article of which he did not understand much. Salim thanked his cousin warmly for the help he had given him and wished him a happy life in the great country of France.

Carlos Fuentes was very happy with his new name and the beauty of Amsterdam made him happy too. Fuentes wasted no time. He joined classes to learn Dutch and promised himself he would not speak Arabic from then on, or mix with Arabs or Iraqis whatever happened in life. 'Had enough of misery, backwardness, death, shit, piss and camels,' he said to himself. In the first year of his new life Fuentes let nothing pass without comparing it with the state of affairs in his original country, sometimes in the form of a question, sometimes as an exclamation. He would walk down the street muttering to himself sulkily and enviously: 'Look how clean the streets are! Look at the toilet seat, it's sparkling clean! Why can't we eat like them? We gobble down our food as though it's about to disappear. If this girl wearing a short skirt and showing her legs were now walking across Eastern Gate Square, she would disappear in an instant. She would only have to walk ten yards and the ground would swallow her up. Why are the trees so green and beautiful, as though they're washed with water every day? Why can't we be peaceful like them? We live in houses like pig sties while their houses are warm, safe and colourful. Why do they respect dogs as much as humans? Why do we masturbate twenty-four hours a day? How can we get a decent government like theirs?' Everything Carlos Fuentes saw amazed him and humiliated him at the same time, from the softness of the toilet paper in Holland to the parliament building protected only by security cameras.

Carlos Fuentes's life went on as he had planned it. Every day he made progress in burying his identity and his past. He always scoffed at the immigrants and other foreigners who did not respect the rules of Dutch life and who complained all the time. He called them 'retarded gerbils'. They work in restaurants illegally, they don't pay taxes and they don't respect any law. They are Stone Age savages. They hate the Dutch, who have fed and housed them. He felt he was the only one who deserved to be adopted by this compassionate and tolerant country, and that the Dutch government should expel all those who did not learn the language properly and anyone who committed the slightest misdemeanour, even crossing the street in violation of the safety code. Let them go shit there in their shitty countries.

After learning Dutch in record time, to the surprise of everyone who knew him, Carlos Fuentes worked non-stop, paid his taxes and refused to live on welfare. The highlight of his efforts to integrate his mind and spirit into Dutch society came when he acquired a goodhearted Dutch girlfriend who loved and respected him. She weighed 90 kilos and had childlike features, like a cartoon character. Fuentes tried hard to treat her as a sensitive and liberated man would, like a

Western man, in fact a little more so. Of course he always introduced himself as someone of Mexican origin whose father had left his country and settled in Iraq to work as an engineer with the oil companies. Carlos liked to describe the Iraqi people as an uncivilised and backward people who did not know what humanity means. 'They are just savage clans,' he would say.

Because of his marriage to a Dutch woman, his proficiency in Dutch, his enrolment in numerous courses on Dutch culture and history, and the fact that he had no legal problems or criminal record in his file, he was able to obtain Dutch citizenship sooner than other immigrants could even dream of and Carlos Fuentes decided to celebrate every year the anniversary of the day he became a Dutch national. Fuentes felt that his skin and blood had changed for ever and that his lungs were now breathing real life. To strengthen his determination he would always repeat: 'Yes, give me a country that treats me with respect, so that I can worship it all my life and pray for it.' That's how things were until the dream problem began and everything fell to pieces, or as they say, proverbs and old adages do not wear out, it's only man that wears out. The wind did not blow fair for Fuentes. The first of the dreams was grim and distressing. In the dream he was unable to speak Dutch. He was standing in front of his Dutch boss and speaking to him in an Iraqi dialect, which caused him great concern and a horrible pain in his head. He would wake up soaked in sweat, then burst into tears. At first he thought they were just fleeting dreams that would inevitably pass. But the dreams continued to assail him without mercy. In his dreams he saw a group of children in the poor district where he was born, running after him and making fun of his new name. They were shouting after him and clapping: 'Carlos the coward, Carlos the sissy, Carlos the silly billy.' These irritating dreams evolved night after night into terrifying nightmares. One night he dreamt that he had planted a car bomb in the centre of Amsterdam. He was standing in the courtroom, ashamed and embarrassed. The judges were strict and would not let him speak Dutch, with intent to humiliate and degrade him. They fetched him an Iraqi translator who asked him not to speak in his incomprehensible rustic accent, which added to his agony and distress.

Fuentes began to sit in the library for hours looking through books about dreams. On his first visit he came across a book called *The Forgotten Language* by Erich Fromm. He did not understand much of it and he did not like the opinions of the writer, which he could not fully grasp because he had not even graduated from middle school. 'This is pure bullshit,' Fuentes said as he read Fromm's book: 'We are free when we are asleep, in fact freer than we are when awake... We may resemble angels in that we are not subject to the laws of reality. During sleep the realm of necessity recedes and gives way to the realm of freedom. The existence of the ego becomes the only reference point for thoughts and feelings.'

Feeling a headache, Fuentes put the book back. How can we be free when we cannot control our dreams? What nonsense! Fuentes asked the librarian if there were any simple books on dreams. The librarian did not understand his question properly or else she wanted to show off how cultured and well-read she was on the subject. She told him of a book about the connection between dreams and food and how one sleeps, then she started to give him more information and advice. She also directed him to a library which had specialist magazines on the mysteries of the world of dreams.

Fuentes's wife had noticed her husband's strange behaviour, as well as the changes in his eating and sleeping habits and in when he went into and came out of the bathroom. Fuentes no longer, for example, ate sweet potato, having previously liked it in all its forms. He was always buying poultry meat, which was usually expensive. Of course his wife did not know he had read that eating any root vegetable would probably be the cause of dreams related to a person's past and roots. Eating the roots of plants has an effect different from that of eating fish, which lives in water, or eating the fruits of trees. Fuentes would sit at the table chewing each piece of food like a camel because he had read that chewing it well helps to get rid of nightmares. He had read nothing about poultry meat, for example, but he just guessed that eating the fowls of the air might bring about dreams that were happier and more liberated.

In all his attempts to better integrate his dreams with his new life, he would veer between what he imagined and the information he found in books. In the end he came to this idea: his ambition went beyond getting rid of troublesome dreams; he had to control the dreams, to modify them, purge them of all their foul air and integrate them with the salubrious rules of life in Holland. The dreams must learn the new language of the country so that they could incorporate new images and ideas. All the old gloomy and miserable faces had to go. So Fuentes read more and more books and magazines about the mysteries of sleep and dreams according to a variety of approaches and philosophies. Fuentes also gave up sleeping naked and touching his wife's naked skin. In bed he began to wear a thick woollen overcoat, which gave rise to arguments with his wife, and so he had to go to the sitting room and sleep on the sofa. Nakedness attracts the sleeper to the zone of childhood, that's what he read too. Every day at 12.05 exactly he would go and have a bath and after coming out of the bathroom he would sit at the kitchen table and take some drops of jasmine oil. Before going to bed at night he would write down on a piece of paper the main calmative foodstuffs which he would buy the following day. This state of affairs went on for more than a month and Fuentes did not achieve good results. But he was patient and his will was invincible. As the days passed he started to perform mysterious secret rituals: he would dye his hair and his toenails green and sleep on his stomach repeating obscure words. One night he painted his face like an American Indian, slept wearing diaphanous orange pyjamas and put under his pillow three feathers taken from various birds.

Fuentes's dignity did not permit him to tell his wife what was happening to him. He believed it was his problem and he could overcome it, since in the past he had survived the most trying and miserable conditions. In return his wife was more indulgent of his eccentric behaviour, because she had not forgotten how kind and generous he was. She decided to give him another chance before intervening and putting an end to what was happening. On one beautiful summer's night Carlos Fuentes was sleeping in a military uniform with a toy plastic rifle by his side. As soon as he began to dream, a wish he had long awaited came true for the first time: he realised in his dream that he was dreaming. This was exactly what he had been seeking, to activate his conscious mind inside the dream so that he could sweep out all the rubbish of the unconscious. In the dream he was standing in front of the door to an old building which looked as though it had been ravaged by fire in its previous life. The building was in central Baghdad. What annoyed him was seeing things through the telescopic sights of the rifle he was holding in his hands. Fuentes broke through the door of the building and went into one flat after another, mercilessly wiping out everyone inside. Even the children did not survive the bursts of bullets. There was screaming, panic and chaos. But Fuentes had strong nerves and picked off his victims with skill and precision. He was worried he might wake up before he had completed his mission, and he thought: 'If I had some hand grenades I could very soon finish the job in this building and move on somewhere else.' But on the sixth floor a surprise hit him when he stormed the first flat and found himself face to face with Salim Abdul Husain! Salim was standing naked next to the window holding a broom stained with blood. With a trembling hand Fuentes aimed his rifle at Salim's head. Salim began to smile and repeated in derision:

'Salim the Dutchman, Salim the Mexican, Salim the Iraqi, Salim the Frenchman, Salim the Indian, Salim the Pakistani, Salim the Nigerian...'

Fuentes's nerves snapped and he panicked. He let out a resounding scream and started to spray Salim Abdul Husain with bullets, but Salim jumped out of the window and not a single bullet hit him.

When Fuentes's wife woke up to the scream and stuck her head out of the window, Carlos Fuentes was dead on the pavement and a pool of blood was spreading slowly under his head. Perhaps Fuentes would have forgiven the Dutch newspapers, which wrote that an Iraqi man had committed suicide at night by jumping from a sixth floor window, instead of writing that a Dutch national had committed suicide. But he will never forgive his brothers, who had his body taken back to Iraq and buried in the cemetery in Najaf. The most beautiful part of the Carlos Fuentes story, however, is the image captured by an amateur photographer who lived close to the scene of the incident. The young man took the picture from a low angle. The police had covered the body and the only part that protruded from under the blue sheet was his outstretched right hand. The picture was in black and white but the stone in the ring on Carlos Fuentes's finger glowed red in the foreground, like a sun in hell.

That Inauspicious Smile

THE SAYING 'THE body must be protected, not the thoughts'* sprang to his mind as he sat on the toilet seat in a Chinese restaurant. He speculated that his mind wanted to solve the puzzle of 'Why that damned smile when I wake up in the morning?' He came out of the toilet and asked for a cup of green tea. He had left the house early that day, before his wife and daughter had got up. From the restaurant he sent his wife a text message saying he had gone out for a short walk and would be back in an hour. Now the hour was running out. He remembered that yesterday she had asked him to buy a new vacuum cleaner on Monday. Just then he noticed two old women sitting in a corner of the restaurant, doing a crossword in the newspaper together. One of them was holding the pen and the other was thinking, with a finger on her nose. The day before the vacuum cleaner had stopped working when he was cleaning the little girl's room. Now he saw the reflection of his smile in the teacup and it turned green. He began to think about the question of thoughts and the body as he watched the two women. Before going into the restaurant he'd witnessed a group of children standing at the traffic lights waiting for green. They stood in two lines with two teachers, one at the front and one at the back. He guessed how many children there were – twelve, of the future hope variety. His mind wagged its tail with delight. They would no doubt be doctors, engineers, murderers, poets, alcoholics and unemployed people, twelve children being the new cover of an old story. His mind slowly moved forward and he began to smell the stench of death. Those are our children and the ones who will visit our graves, he said.

* Attributed to Albert Camus.

83

Twelve ideas crossing the street, cheerful and energetic. They are the powerhouse of the future. He stood up and headed to the bathroom again. He washed his face for the tenth time but the smile was still stuck there. If he had not had trouble with fantasies in the past, he would have behaved like any sensible man, looked in the mirror and said: 'Impossible'. But he was used to surprises and his experiences had taught him not to waste time looking for reasons for his predicaments and to look for the emergency exit instead. His mind guessed that the smile had come to him from a previous dream. It was a naïve, cinematic dream which had absolutely nothing to do with his past:

He kisses her on the lips and tries to climb the stairs, then sits back down at the foot of them. He smiles and leans his head against the wall. She brushes her teeth in the kitchen and shouts out to him, asking him to bring the bed sheet. She wants to wash it. But now he's going down a well like a feather tumbling through the air. He is far from the light, a dead man who doesn't hear her last call. Four years after this stair incident the woman dies. They find her lying on the kitchen table with the toothbrush in her hand and, on the brush, a piece of meat the size of an ant.

Shall we say that, after the woman brushes her teeth, the rays of the sun stream through the window, or that the rain is beating the windowpane? The same dream recurs every night. There's a need for this ancient music, and yet how many of these timeless death stories have disappeared? What eternal naïvety there is in tales about our beautiful death! These little stories that are pointed like a toothbrush. Why did we contrive to complicate these death stories? A giant shadow poses these questions to the man in the dream.

In the morning the man woke up smiling, then he saw his smile in the mirror. It seemed to have stayed stuck there after the dream. Once, in an unusual discussion with a member of the Association for the Defence of the Luckless, he said:

'I didn't want my wife and daughter to see me smiling like an idiot for no reason. It was an insignificant smile. It was wide but it didn't show my damaged teeth. My lips were sealed like the lips of a clown. I rubbed my face with soap and water but the smile was still stuck there. I brushed my teeth three times but it stayed there like indelible ink. I thought: "Maybe it will disappear as the day proceeds, as the snow melts on a sunny morning." I don't know how such thoughts occurred to me. Then suddenly I felt intensely hot, although the season was winter. I put on a light sports shirt printed on the back with a picture of a black crow standing on a basketball. The ball was marked like a map of the world. I put on a clean pair of jeans and my black winter coat. I resolved to solve the mystery of that smile. The wife and daughter have put up with much – I worry I might drive them mad – because I've had a succession of disasters in this world. I'm not luckless, so stop sticking that stupid label on me.

'The snow was dancing down. It was amazing and beautiful. For the first time the sky was so munificent, when it yielded all these jewels to me. I had known feelings like these before. You wake up and smell a morning, then you think: "Life still suits me." There are disguised moments of sadness which hide in various clothes and smells. You get drunk and weep and think you have cleared away a large rock blocking the channels of your day, which had come to an end with a painful blow. A man I don't know passed close by me, wearing a heavy winter coat, a woollen scarf wrapped around his neck and on his head a black hat on which the snowflakes had gathered. He kept looking and turning towards me with a smile as he walked in the opposite direction. I wanted to return his smile. I passed my fingers along my lips. So I didn't need a new smile. I made do with turning towards him quickly to offer him in return that dream smile of mine.

'I went into the Chinese restaurant to have some tea and check up on the smile in the mirror. I saw two old lesbians doing the crossword puzzle. I sent my wife a second message on my phone telling her I would be back a little late and would go straight to the shops to buy the vacuum cleaner. I had to find a solution for the damned smile. I thought of going to the hospital. Perhaps I'm ill and the smile is just an alarm bell. But instead of that I found myself going into a cinema and buying a ticket. I felt a nasty fever spreading through my body. There were some girls under a large poster of next week's film. What stood out was Dracula's fangs and the blood running down from the corners of his mouth. There was a smile on the face of this monster. The girls sat down as though they were in class at school. All of them gave me stiff looks, with a tinge of fear. Then they smiled in turn, from right to left. I was sitting in front of them. I took off my coat and turned my back on them so that they could clearly see the basketball and the crow. Don't ask me why I did that. Do you have an answer to this damned smile? Then I checked on the features of my face in the mirrors in the foyer. I confess I was somewhat satisfied with this new smile. At least I don't have to contract my face muscles in order to smile, as other people do. I forgot to tell you that one of the old lesbians told me to keep this beautiful smile because the Finns are gloomy in winter and look depressed, which makes the winter darker and more dreary.

'The film was a disgusting fast-paced tear-jerker. The heroine set fire to her house with her husband and children inside. Now she's screaming and sobbing in front of the fire and the neighbours have their fingers on their mouths as though they are about to vomit. The elegant lady sitting near me was drowning in tears. She turned slowly towards me and muttered in shock: "The pig!" I turned to her in disbelief. Then she looked at me again but this time disdainfully. She began to look back and forth like an imbecile between the disaster of the heroine in the film and my beaming face. She looked as though she were revolted and wanted to slap me because of my smile. I wanted to explain to her: "I'm not smiling at what happened to the woman and her house, lady, (although she's a bitch like you). I woke up this morning and found this smile had been forced upon me."

'I ignored the woman and tried to pretend I pitied the woman in the film, who took a revolver out of her belt and fired a bullet into her head amid a crowd of people, who quickly dispersed when the fire engines arrived.

'When the lights came on in the cinema, the elegant lady stood up and insulted me, this time out loud. "Animal, son of a bitch!" she shouted.

'The audience turned towards me but all they did was smile as they looked at my face. Were they smiling at the insult, or at the crow on the ball, or because I answered the woman's insult with my cold smile? I have to get rid of this smile as soon as possible. My wife called me but I lied and said I was still looking for a suitable vacuum cleaner.

'The snow kept falling and it sparkled even more when a light wind rose and made it fall at a slant. I was frightened and confused, thinking that this smile might appear when some disaster happens. What if a bus runs over one of them now and his guts come out of his ass? Surely there would be a panicky crowd. What if they noticed my smile as I joined them in watching this free spectacle? Without doubt they would give me a thorough beating. How would I explain to them that my smile had nothing to do with what had happened? Or who would put up with you smiling in his face when, for example, his baby was dying of hunger in front of his eyes? Could you calmly explain to him that you are smiling in derision at life, which produced this child without reason and then took it away with a kick in the guts, also without reason? Wouldn't the father and mother of this child stab you and tear apart this hard-hearted animal? I hurried off to a bar nearby. The body must be protected, not the thoughts. What if you were to lose control over the inherited communal gestures which unite us in fear and in happiness?

'I felt a stomach pain when I went into the bar, which was suspiciously crowded. The Finns start drinking early in the day. My arrival in the bar set off a smile-fest but the smiles gradually waned and turned into laughs and intermittent comments which were, technically, quick insults. At first I didn't understand why the barman hesitated when I ordered a beer. Then he said: "You should drink up your beer quickly and leave." In turn I looked at the other customers, angry at such an unfriendly reception. What kind of bar is this? I said that out loud but, as you know, I was smiling in spite of myself. Perhaps they had the notion that I was just a tame animal that had taken more than his fair share. There were four young men with shaved heads in black leather jackets. Only then did I realise that this was a neo-Nazi bar. They were making fun of my daring or my stupidity, looking at me between one drink and another and making ugly jokes and insults. Then one of them stood up, took out his cock and waved it in my face. Everyone burst out laughing, including the barman. I thought I would keep myself under control, drink the beer quickly and escape this filthy trap. But I was stupid. I pretended to be brave and indifferent. I sat there like a captain smiling in his ship. But the barman, that son of a whore, asked me to leave at once for fear of problems. Of course I was delighted with this expulsion. And so I left the Nazis' bar like a frightened mouse. It was Sunday and I had thought it was Monday. At least I remembered that and I thought my wife would be angry when she read my text messages. Which electrical goods stores are these that open on Sunday? Now what other lie could I make up to cover my first lie? I thought of going home and confessing everything to my wife. The smile would be proof I was telling the truth. But my feelings were contradictory. Then I entered a small shop, bought six bottles of beer and went to the park. Do I really have bad luck? Or was I born by mistake?

'The streets were empty and the wind was playing havoc and making a racket when it tried to shift things from their place. The wind blew over a price list parked outside a closed restaurant, then it brought along a large cardboard box which flew around like half a dismembered body. There were empty cigarette packets racing each other about. Unconsciously I hummed a tune. I wanted to sing but I did not know which song to choose. I didn't have the words to any song in my head. A slight anxiety came over me. Had the words to songs been sucked out of my memory to this extent? All I could do was make up some little songs. I kept humming in the hope that I would come across some words in a while, but stupid tears came instead of words. The wind blew an empty white bag which passed close to my ear and made me forget the tune. It had frightened me. The bag did a somersault at the junction as though it was deciding which way to go. It rose uncertainly for a moment, then fell in a lurch to the asphalt. This time the wind dragged it along the ground in spite of itself and left it next to the rubbish that had accumulated at the mouth of the street drain.

'I reached the garden thinking about how I had lied to my wife. Definitely she would be convinced I had a date with a woman. Now she would be in a rage, stuffing my clothes into a suitcase in readiness to throw me out.

'When I looked through the thick trees I thought at first that the wind had blown in some other black bags, but in reality it had brought those four young men with shaven heads. With the instinct of an animal I sensed danger. I caught their smell when they came close to me. For no reason I stood up to piss behind a giant tree. Two of them surrounded me on the right and the others on the left. They looked like Guardian Angels. They took out their cocks and all of them pissed with vigour like donkeys that had not pissed for years. As they pissed they looked at me stiffly and contemptuously because of my cock, which out of fear had not released a single drop. I was an easy prey, and cowardly. The noise of their piss gushing out filled the air, like a waterfall cascading in the darkness. The wind died down, or slowed down to make space for the symphony of their pissing. The smell of it drifted up to my brain like poisonous nerve gas, or perhaps the wind wanted to give the sky a free look.

'Everything was over with lightning speed. In just a few minutes they gave vent to all possible animal instincts, giving me a thorough beating. Then they ran off, as though the wind had picked them up, hidden them in the folds of its solemn cloak and gone back to work after the youths had carried out their mission to perfection. I was bleeding from my ear, my nose, my teeth and my eye, and from the blocked nostrils of my soul as well. I tried to get up. I wished that this wind, a slave to the sky in blind obedience and allegiance, would pick me up too but it didn't. It was sweeping up everything but my empty body, which lay bleeding by the tree, as though what had happened was part of a humorous story full of banal scrapes. I saw empty bags of every colour and shape. They were hovering around me at crazy speeds, as though they were making me a special offer of leftover bones, times and places. They did not seem happy with me, nor did the force blowing them. A torn grey bag flew past and I realised it was my mother's shawl. A burnt brain flew by on giant wings. A shoal of fish swam past carrying scraps of a young girl's flesh. The flying vipers of economic sanctions flew by, wrapped around their food of humans and dreams. All my wife's underwear went past, one pair dripping blood, another semen, the next one ink and so on. My old notebooks passed by, clapping their covers. Scorpions in a bottle went past, my summer shirts, medicines which had expired and cartons of baby milk. Bread went by on wings of shit. Poems passed, pissing on themselves like disabled children. With their savage dogs the guards on the borders I had walked across went past. My cross-eyed brother who wears the turban of an imam. My severed and bloodied fingers flew by, my daughter Mariam in her pram, disfigured because I loved her too much. My wife went by, playing a trumpet that screeched like an owl.

'My whole life passed page by page, all the jams and scrapes I had been through, page after page. Even when I closed my eyes it didn't stop. Pain and vertigo had me in their power. The pages went past in the darkness, white page after page.'

In the evening the man was laid out on a bed in hospital, smiling at his wife and daughter, who was holding a beautiful bunch of flowers.

'Why are you smiling like that, daddy?' Mariam asked in surprise.